MW00463898

Deep Flakes Christmas

A Nisse Visit

Joy Ann Ribar

ten16press.com – Waukesha, WI

Deep Flakes Christmas: A Nisse Visit
Copyrighted © 2020 Joy Ann Ribar
ISBN 978-1-64538-185-3
First Edition

Deep Flakes Christmas: A Nisse Visit
by Joy Ann Ribar

For information, please contact:

ten16press.com
Waukesha, WI

Edited by Kay Rettenmund
Cover design by Tom Heffron

For all the Believers, but especially our grandchildren: Will, Kaleb, Layla, Zoren, Juliana, Astoria, Tesla, Emberlynn, Vox, Alexandra, Miro, Natalie, Oden, Zedekiah, Julia, and Ophelia. You bring the magic into our lives! And, welcome to the fold, Leah and Drew.

Chapter One

"Three weeks 'til Christmas Eve—we got this, right, Carmen?" Frankie Champagne, Bubble and Bake owner, sat at the bar in the wine lounge area of the bake shop, probing her business partner, pen in hand, poised over a yellow legal pad.

Carmen's lackluster response was barely a verbal mutter. The business was closed Mondays, but the partners met to review the week's agenda and prepare a list for the market in Madison. Carmen's old paneled van trekked to the Mid Winter Market in the renovated Garver Feed Mill most Mondays like clockwork, arriving early for the best offerings of the season.

"I just don't understand why you agreed to take on so much, Frankie. Sometimes you're the Queen of Impossible." Carmen's brow was furrowed, but she grinned at Frankie, who shrugged.

"Didn't have much choice, Carmen. Somebody had to step up to save the local holiday season." Frankie held out her right hand, ready to count off her to-do list with her left index finger, but paused at Carmen's warning look.

"I know, I know. You don't have to be so dramatic, Frankie. Bubble and Bake isn't the only business in town.

You don't have to take on everything, just saying." Carmen smiled at Frankie's slightly offended expression.

Deep Lakes was preparing for its annual holiday season festivities, but this year, there was a hitch. Mayor Adele Lundgren was called away to Chicago to help her daughter, whose baby decided to arrive a month early. "Not to worry," Adele told the chamber of commerce members; she had already enacted Plan B: the city council chairman had all the necessary information and contacts to proceed as planned.

Except that Council Chairman Hastrich was unexpectedly called away to Arizona where his elderly mother had fallen, dislocated her shoulder and broken her arm, and would need her son's assistance indefinitely. Adele didn't know this, and nobody was going to interrupt her motherly duty to tell her.

Instead, the council looked to the city clerk for Plan C. Except, the city clerk, Kelley LeVay, was new in town, only arriving in Deep Lakes in June, after the old clerk retired. Certainly the retired clerk, Annette Jones, could pick up the reins to move the plans along. Except, Annette was an ocean away from Deep Lakes, celebrating her 50th wedding anniversary in Hawaii and wouldn't be returning until after the new year.

Having exhausted many letters in the alphabet conjuring alternate plans, the city council looked to the chamber for one of its members to step up and take charge. Although Frankie swore she hadn't volunteered, the other members declared she was perfect for the task: organized, detail-oriented and energetic.

Chamber President Stuart Ness, owner of Ness Travel Agency, was up to his eyeballs in trying to coax a cable travel network to film an episode in Deep Lakes next summer. Stuart was all about promoting tourism and hoped to turn Deep Lakes from quaint to mega destination. Along with that project, the agency was absorbed in finalizing travel packages for everyone wanting to escape winter after the holidays. January was a bustling month for vacations to warmer climes. Frankie wasn't even a chamber officer, but with Stuart's nomination, the remaining members jumped on the suggestion like a New Yorker on a taxi.

Frankie had to admit she welcomed the distraction that organizing the holiday events brought. She still struggled to fully immerse herself in holiday glee. She went through all the motions of celebrating a heartfelt Christmas, but inwardly, she had abandoned her holiday whimsy. Since her painful divorce from Rick, Frankie had donned a mask of good cheer for their young daughters every year. Yet, every Christmas Eve, she found herself crying as she watched a classic movie after the girls went to bed, saturated with loneliness. Both daughters were adults, but Frankie still felt the holidays were lackluster. Carmen had advised her not to spend so much time with her head in the clouds, waiting for the Christmas Fairy to descend with the perfect Christmas. But, Frankie the idealist, still looked for the Christmas Fairy.

Frankie gulped the rich holiday blend coffee, inhaling its aroma. "All I really need to do here is get the ball rolling. If only I had last year's committee list . . . I suspect most of the same business owners from last year are on the same committees this year. Sadly, for now, I'll just have to call around. Guess it's going to be hit and miss."

Carmen nodded, frowning at the prospect of having to cold call all the town businesses. "Same events?" she asked.

Frankie began checking off the list on her fingers. "December 7th marks the beginning of Deep Lakes After Dark with extended shopping hours. All of the businesses are expected to have their store windows decorated by 5 p.m. the day before for the judges to award prizes."

Carmen jumped in, a note of urgency in her voice. "That means we need everyone to get decorating here this week, Frankie. The 6th is Thursday."

"True. I'll see if Jovie is available to help. I already told Chloe to be here every day she doesn't have schoolwork." Frankie made a note on the next page of the tablet.

Jovie Luedtke was a local woman who helped out at the bakery and at Shamrock Floral when needed. Both jobs gave her a break from her overbearing mother, who always found a reason to keep Jovie at home.

Chloe was the shop intern from Madison College, learning the ropes of working the bakery scene before graduation later in the month. When she came to Bubble and Bake last May, Frankie and Carmen weren't sure she was going to work out. A tough city girl of only 21, Chloe arrived sporting a skull and rose tattoo on her shoulder, along with a gigantic chip that possibly grew there from a hard-knock life. She was shorter than average and built like a boxer. As part of Chloe's training, Frankie requested she look in the mirror and practice smiling, since Chloe's smiles were sneers at best. But, after a few months in Deep Lakes, Chloe looked happier, less intense, and had picked up on how to chit-chat with customers.

"I guess I can ask my mother to help, too," Frankie added.

"Good idea. Your mom has a great eye for design. Besides, she'd be hurt if you didn't ask her," Carmen said, knowingly.

Frankie knew Carmen was right about her mother. Peggy Champagne worked at the wine lounge every Thursday night and Sunday afternoon to help her daughter, often chiming in with ideas to promote the shop. Frankie appreciated her mother's support, and she knew Peggy appreciated staying busy after signing over the Champagne construction company to James, Frankie's brother.

Peggy had been the financial manager for the company she and Charlie Champagne ran for 35 years until Charlie passed away five years ago. Frankie missed her dad terribly; the father-daughter duo were like bacon and eggs. Frankie wished her relationship with Peggy was just as smooth and easy, but it just wasn't. Frankie supposed being the only girl among the five children created added pressure for her, trying to live up to expectations, some real, some imagined.

"Mostly imagined, I imagine," came a buzzy whisper in Frankie's right ear. A firefly, looking like an angel with a glowing halo, floated midair. Frankie's inner voices were a dichotomy of her conscience. She couldn't pinpoint the catalyst of their first appearance, but accepted them just the same. She called the firefly angel, The Golden One or Goldie. Naturally, Goldie sounded like Peggy Champagne.

"We are, how you say, a manifestation of your thoughts. We keep you from talking to yourself, Cara Mia." The Pirate firefly materialized on Frankie's left earlobe, cooing like a sultry dove. His cocked hat looked whimsical and so did his striped stockings, but his voice was deep and sensuous like Antonio Banderas's. It was clear Frankie favored The Pirate over The Golden One.

"Earth to Frankie," Carmen nudged her friend. "Let's finalize the shopping list, so I can head out. Are we still going to the winery later?"

Frankie nodded again, adding another note to her list. "Thanks for reminding me. Besides the Christmas decorations, I'm going to grab a few more cases of Winter Dreams and Hygge Holiday. They always sell out by New Year's."

Bountiful Fruits, Frankie's vineyard, crafted two holiday wines: Winter Dreams was a smooth, semi-sweet white made from Brianna and LaCrescent grapes, with a surprising almond finish, while Hygge Holiday was a deep red blend, also semi-sweet, crafted in the frizzante style, meaning it was slightly effervescent. Both were designed to please most palates and accompany most celebrations. Both held up well beside hearty holiday comfort foods of the Midwest.

Carmen dashed out the back door before Frankie could sidetrack her further.

By the time Carmen returned, snow was falling in wet clusters of flakes, and Frankie had called most of the business owners to serve on committees, leaving voicemail messages with many of them, unfortunately. A flatbread pizza with caramelized onions, baby bella mushrooms, smashed garlic, and gouda cheese was roasting in the oven.

"Wow, I bet you could hear my stomach growl from the alley," Carmen laughed, toting in two stacked boxes of produce. "Come help me unload the rest. It's going to take a few trips. I loaded up in bulk this time, just in case."

The walk-in cooler was ample, and since the holidays were approaching, Carmen doubled up on things that would keep well: cheeses, butter, eggs, deli meats and certain produce. Grinning from ear to ear, Carmen held up two sacks, like a bank robber with a jackpot. "I snagged a sack of hickory nuts and butter nuts, too, before they sold out."

Frankie gave a little clap of excitement. Only while

their supplies lasted could they bake sweet and savory treats with Wisconsin-harvested nuts. Both varieties were expensive because of the intensive labor to hull the nuts, crack the hard shells, and dig out the nut pieces. And, they had to be cured and properly stored during autumn before being ready for use. "We'll store them in the walk-in, too, then plan which goodies we'll make with them."

After a quick lunch, Frankie and Carmen grabbed shovels from the alley and did a quick cleanup of the sidewalk in front of the store, although snow continued falling.

"Come on, Frankie, let's get out to the winery before it gets dark. We can take the van. It's warmed up and has a lot less snow to clean off of it than your SUV." Carmen had already climbed in the driver's side of the van, started it up, and set the wipers in motion to clear off most of the snow. Frankie grabbed the snow brush to clean the back windshield, jumped in the van, and the two were off.

Bountiful Fruits was only a few miles out of town, but the snow-covered roads made navigation slower. The van wasn't nearly as good in the snow as the SUV, and it slid around some on the curves of County K. When they turned onto Blackbird Marsh Road, there were no longer any tire tracks to follow, and Carmen had to gauge the width of the road by trees and mailboxes along the shoulder. They almost missed the driveway up to the winery, since the sign was caked with snow, but Frankie pointed it out just in time.

Carmen parked the van on the concrete slab next to the winery entrance. Frankie sent Carmen to retrieve cases of the holiday wines while she trudged down to the storage building where tubs of Christmas decorations spent the off-season.

Frankie opened the heavy door and spied the utility carts lined up along the wall. Smiling, she climbed the steps to the loft, located the bins, and reminded herself to walk carefully with only one tub at a time. Frankie wasn't graceful by any stretch of the imagination and had a lot of bruises to show for it, so she was thankful the carts were at the ready. She managed to cram the four tubs onto the wagon, shoved open the heavy door once more, and trudged back through the thick snow, the wagon resisting her every move.

Carmen was loading the last case of wine and tried to run toward Frankie to help, but landed on her bottom partway down the hillside. Frankie dropped the wagon handle, causing it to slide backwards, but she managed to thrust herself backward to grab the handle, tumbling to her knees in the snow. Both women couldn't stop laughing. Carmen rose, plodded her way to Frankie, who was now leaning against the loaded wagon, laughing herself silly. The two manhandled the wagon up the hill to the waiting van.

"Thanks for coming to my rescue, Carmie. I think I need to pee—too much laughing." The comment started a fresh round of chortles. "I'll be right back."

But, when Frankie got back to the van, Carmen was scowling. "Van won't start. It won't even turn over."

The two weighed their options. Bountiful was shut down for the holidays, on hiatus until mid-January. The equipment had been thoroughly sanitized, and the workers were on vacation. Frankie's brother, James, lived just up the road from the vineyard, but was out of town visiting his wife's relatives in Minnesota for an early holiday gathering. Carmen's husband, Ryan, was likely in the middle of afternoon sheep duties and out of cell phone range.

"Well, it's either a tow truck or Alonzo. What do you think?" Frankie wasn't sure she should take advantage of her long-standing friendship with Alonzo Goodman, the county sheriff. She hoped Carmen, the more levelheaded of the two women, would weigh in with the best decision.

"Call Alonzo. If he can't get out here, he'll at least know someone to dispatch. Let's go inside, huh? It's getting colder out here." Carmen pulled her hood around her tightly while the wind whipped snow in her face. Frankie hunkered deeper inside her own parka. Their wet blue jeans made them feel even more chilled.

Back inside the wine lab, Frankie punched in Alonzo's personal number, happy that he picked up almost immediately.

"And how's my favorite baker?" Alonzo's voice sounded cheery on the other end. Frankie wondered if the consummate bachelor was seeing someone or just welcomed a break from the quiet monotony of the post-tourist season in Deep Lakes.

"I'm okay, Lon, except that Carmen and I are stuck at the vineyard. The van won't start," Frankie sounded more frazzled than she thought she felt, making her question just how many balls she could juggle at once.

"Just sit tight, I'll send someone out. We're starting to get traffic incident calls now that the snowstorm is really cooking. You know how it is; people forget how to drive every winter and have to learn the hard way." Midwesterners know the winter season doesn't follow the calendar, with first snows arriving as early as October some years. The fact it was almost December, and Deep Lakes hadn't recorded a significant snowfall, was unusual.

"Thanks, Lon. I guess we're overdue. This one looks like it's going to be a doozy, too. Stay safe out there," Frankie added.

It was almost a half-hour later when a brown Ford F250 rolled up the Bountiful Fruits driveway and halted on the thick snow-covered slab next to the van. Frankie didn't recognize the driver, who was mostly concealed by his fully zipped navy-blue parka and gray trapper hat with ear flaps. Still, Frankie could see their rescuer was sporting a genuine smile he presented when she opened the door.

"Hello. You must be Frankie Champagne. I'm the county coroner, Garrett Iverson." Garrett removed his heavy thermal gloves to shake Frankie's hand.

Coroner? Frankie gave a little snort. "What, did you come here to pronounce the van dead?" Sometimes Frankie spoke impulsively, an attribute she claimed was inherited from her quick-witted MéMé, her Irish grandmother.

Garrett laughed in spite of himself and quipped back, "Matter of fact, I even have the tools of resuscitation if needed." He held up a case containing jumper cables. "No respectable first responder would be without them."

Lucky for Frankie and Carmen, Garrett's heavy duty pick-up was just what the van's dead battery needed, although the engine gave a half-hearted chug at best. He followed the women into town straight to the auto parts store where, $175 later, Garrett installed the new battery right in the store parking lot.

Remembering her manners, Frankie showed her gratitude to the coroner for all of his help that afternoon. She opened one case of Hygge Holiday wine and handed a bottle to Garrett, noticing the man's good looks for the first time. Perhaps a little older than Frankie, Garrett's dark hair was streaked in silver but was lush and wavy near his ears and neckline.

His features were pleasant, making her feel warm and trusting. But his eyes were his standout feature for sure: kind, sparkling with humor and expression, the color of caramelized sugar.

"Just like creme brulee," Frankie said out loud.

Garrett thanked Frankie for the wine. "You said this

wine tastes like creme brulee?" Garrett cocked an eyebrow, uncertainly.

It took a few more seconds for Frankie to recover. "No, this is a red blend; it goes well with everything, smooth and a little sparkly, which is how I'm hoping the holidays in Deep Lakes will be."

Garrett was still holding his hat in one hand, the wine bottle in the other, but he said goodbye, placing his hat over his heart in an endearing gesture, nodding and smiling at the red-haired spitfire. Garrett couldn't help thinking Frankie Champagne was a red blend in her own right—goes well with everything, smooth and sparkly.

Chapter Two

Frankie slept fitfully; her to-do list cartwheeled around her mind and failed to organize itself into something manageable. Every time Frankie thought she had dismissed the whirling dervish of tasks, the ever-annoying jingle, "Twelve Days of Christmas," intruded in her thoughts, and she had to begin again. Finally, she turned on her nightstand light, opened the stand's top drawer, and pulled out a small notebook and pen. *Might as well make an actual list of what needs to be done tomorrow instead of swimming around in this stew,* she thought.

Item one: Decorate the shop. Hopefully this could be accomplished with her shop helpers and she would have little to do with it. Check.

Item two: Clear off city skating rink. That would probably just take a phone call to public works. On the same subject, the area surrounding the rink needs to be decorated with lights and displays, so the city's decorations must be found and hauled to Spurgeon Park. Also, someone needs to be in charge of decorating the rink area. Check.

Item three: Organize the Christmas parade. Frankie had not been part of the parade in the past and had no idea who was in charge of it. She might have to call Adele. Frankie balked at the idea of disturbing Adele's motherly and grandmotherly duties. Surely the parade floats and performers were standard each year, right? Bubble and Bake always helped with the tree lighting ceremony after the parade, so she never actually saw the downtown spectacle. More information needed. Check.

Item four: The tree lighting ceremony. That event usually ran like clockwork. Snowy Ridge Christmas Trees provided the mega-sized spruce and delivered it to Spurgeon Park a few days early. The public works department and firemen would string it with thousands of lights and top it with the North Star topper, a multi-dimensional star woven together with gold and silver metal strands accented by shiny crystals and white lights. Caught up in the memory of Christmas trees past, the pen fell from Frankie's hand as she settled into a quiet sleep.

A few hours later, the morning bakery sales completed, Frankie was perched in the Bubble and Bake kitchen, mixing up the first batch of Christmas cookie dough of the season. Last year, while she watched a cooking show, a pure black cookie that resembled a lump of coal piqued her interest, and she decided she would try to replicate the recipe. Now, the idea of a naughty lump of coal cookie made her grin. She had ordered the special black cocoa required for the experiment and began adding different ingredients for lumps. Large nut pieces, chocolate chunks, broken sandwich cookies of various flavors, chocolate dipped pretzels, broken peanut butter cups, or thin mints were some of the lumpy goodies distributed among different bowls of dough. Soon, she would have a kitchen filled with guinea pigs for the trial.

The annoying to-do list from Frankie's nearly sleepless night sat on the counter, vying with the cookie dough for her attention. *All right, already, I'll make calls while the cookies bake, and the laundry dries, I suppose,* she thought. Frankie was accustomed to doing three things at once when possible.

Her foremost occupation for years had been single mom. Along with the usual trials of motherhood, Frankie was the sole breadwinner for her little family, meaning she found herself with a full plate as the norm. Once her daughters were grown, she couldn't bear having an empty plate, so she made room for other occupations. Sometimes, she wondered if she constantly kept moving as a way to cope with being left to raise her children alone.

With the cookie trays in the oven, Frankie tapped in the number for public works. Head employee Ted Lennon picked up immediately, sounding a little harried.

"Hi, Ted, this is Frankie Champagne at Bubble and Bake. How's it going?" Frankie tried not to launch right into business if possible and found that small talk was a good warm-up for wanting a favor.

Ted had worked for public works some 20 years and knew the ins and outs of all things related to the streets, parks, and public areas of the community, but today was not Ted's day. "Hi-ya Frankie. You're catching me at a bad time. The waterworks are froze up down at City Hall, so it's all hands on deck trying to get 'er fixed. Did ya need something?"

Oh, boy, Frankie had a knack for walking into problem situations, but this was one she couldn't help fix. "Actually, Ted, as soon as you can, we need to get the decorations for the ice skating rink hauled to the park. And, speaking of the rink, we're going to need it cleared of snow for the Christmas festivities." Frankie was chewing on one finger, hoping she hadn't overstepped.

"Well, if you want the decorations, come on down and pick up my keys. Grab a couple of people and a truck, and you can haul them to the park yourself. That's what the planners did last year, anyway." Ted's voice sounded strained, and Frankie could hear banging nearby. "As soon as we can, we'll get up to clear the rink. Maybe you can wrangle some kids to keep it shoveled through the holidays?"

"Is that what usually happens—volunteers keep the rink shoveled?" Frankie felt discouraged as she added more tasks to her list, after Ted's confirmation about the volunteers. She wished him good luck and signed off, figuring nobody else at City Hall was going to be able to help her out today.

Frankie placed a second call to her foremost source for local information: her mother.

"Hi, Mom. I'm hoping you can help me with some

names. Do you remember who worked on the ice rink part of the Christmas festival?"

"I'm just fine, Francine, and I hope you're doing well, too." Peggy sometimes took the opportunity to remind her daughter of the importance of manners. "I'm quite sure Bonnie Fleisner has been in charge of the ice rink decorating and set up for the festival the past few years." As if Frankie's mother could see Frankie rolling her eyes and frowning on the other end of the line, she added, "Be nice when you talk to her, Frankie. Bonnie's not all bad."

Truth be told, Fleisner's Hardware was just a couple doors down from Bubble and Bake and squatted on Sterling Creek across from the bakery. Of course, with Frankie living right above her shop, Bonnie Fleisner didn't miss much of what was going on in Frankie's backyard. Bonnie was as bossy as she was nosy, considered herself an authority on all city matters, and was often mistaken in her version of events.

"Maybe you could call Bonnie about getting the ice rink decorations, Mom?" Frankie was hopeful but doubted her mother would come to her rescue.

"I'm sorry, Honey, but I've got my hands full with the historical society's role in the festivities. We need to find a sleigh and horses for starters. Sleigh rides are going to be part of the tree lighting ceremony this year. Did I tell you we're trying to find Victorian costumes and period music, too?" The tree lighting always featured live music and caroling.

"That's okay, Mom. Everyone's busy. Will you be able to come down this week to help decorate the shop windows? We sure could use your finesse." Frankie meant the compliment. Peggy Champagne had style.

"Of course, I'd be happy to. Call me if you need any other information on the festival. Good luck, Dear."

She stared at her festival list with dismay—so much to do and, in this case, her multitasking penchant wasn't going to serve any purpose. Each item on her list required phone calls, and those could only be made one at a time. First, Frankie figured she'd head over to Fleisner's as soon as her bakery crew arrived.

The last pans of coal lump cookies were baking, warming the kitchen considerably, so Frankie slid open the window a crack. Looking out the back window at Sterling Creek, she noticed her winter birds had emptied the suet and sunflower seeds. Snowstorms conjured extra birds at the feeders, and yesterday's heavy snowfall was no exception.

Frankie headed out the back door, opened the birdseed bucket, and scooped a container full of seeds. A bright red color caught her eye, and she turned, smiling, expecting to feast her eyes upon a beautiful male cardinal. Instead, she saw what looked like a bobbing red pointy hat rounding the corner into the alleyway between her shop and the real estate office.

Frankie wasn't able to get down her back steps fast enough and missed whatever she thought she saw. The alley was empty, except for a small ball of fur, curled up on the pavement. Frankie set down the birdseed and approached the furry bundle stealthily. Peering up at Frankie with sad, dark golden eyes was a semi-frozen silver cat, barely able to move. Frankie carefully gathered the silver mound into her arms, the birdseed now forgotten, and trotted back to the bakery kitchen, setting the kitty near the ovens to warm up.

Bubble and Bake often hosted guest cats from the local vet as a form of community service. Shop customers might fall in love with the visitor and give him or her a forever home. Now Frankie retrieved some kitty kibble and set a dish out for the frozen feline, but the cat showed no interest.

Frankie jumped into action, grabbing a shop towel fresh from the dryer and wrapping it around the lethargic cat. She warmed a little milk and offered it with coaxing coos. The cat lapped a little, closing its eyes as Frankie pulled embedded ice out of the kitty's paws. "You poor little thing. I bet somebody is missing you." Frankie looked, but didn't find an ID of any kind. "Maybe you lost your collar in the snow, hmm?"

"Better add a trip to the vet to your list this morning," The Golden One tsk-ed, and Frankie reluctantly admitted that Goldie was right. One more thing she didn't have time for, naturally.

A few minutes later though, Carmen breezed into the back door with Chloe and a stranger on Carmen's heels.

Pointing a thumb at the young woman, Chloe introduced her. "This is my friend, Sharmaine. She's in the baking program too and graduating with me. My car wouldn't start, so I asked her to drive me, and she's willing to work for free just to learn."

Frankie and Carmen brightened, welcoming the extra help with open arms.

"Glad to have your help, Sharmaine. We've got a lot of Christmas baking and decorating to do," Frankie began, holding out her hand to shake Sharmaine's firmly.

"Plus a whole lot of other holiday projects, so an extra pair of hands are always needed. Thanks for coming," Carmen finished, reaching out her own hand to greet Sharmaine.

"I'm glad you're not mad that I'm here. Chloe said you wouldn't be, but you never know. I just want to learn at a real bakery." Sharmaine explained she'd been an intern at a bake shop in Madison that went out of business after the summer season, leaving Sharmaine without the experience that would help her attain a job in the field after graduation.

"Chloe, you know the ropes. The list for today is next to the window. Why don't you pick something, show Sharmaine how we make it and where to find things in the kitchen. Then, you can go from there." Frankie was smiling as Chloe dove right in, handing Sharmaine a shop apron.

Meanwhile, Carmen pulled her hair into a tight pony tail and tucked it under her shirt collar, as was her custom, when she spied the small furry lump snoozing by the ovens. "Frankie, who's that? New shop visitor from Dr. Sadie?"

"Oh, geez, I almost forgot. I found this poor frozen creature in the alley. I need to get her to the vet to have her checked out." Frankie filled in the details about the silver kitty, including her efforts to warm her up and get her to eat.

Carmen nodded, not surprised to find her business partner taking in a stray critter. Two of a kind, softhearted Carmen opened up the farm to strays, too, welcoming abandoned cats to keep the mice and moles under control. Carmen played nurse to many other foundlings that her twin boys, Kyle and Carlos, sometimes dragged home, including an abandoned fawn whose mother was killed by a car. The fawn bedded down with the O'Connor's lambs, eating the same food until it was old enough to be on its own in the wild.

"Okay. You go. I'll get going on the yeast dough so it can rest, then make the wedding cake cookies while these two work on cut-out cookies. When Jovie gets here, I'll put her on thumbprints," Carmen rattled off the itinerary with military precision, easing Frankie's worries about their to-do list.

Frankie offered Carmen a quick hug, zipped up her parka, and scurried to the hall closet to retrieve the cat carrier, always on hand for shop kitty visitors. "I guess it's a good thing we're between shop cats, huh," she said, "this one might be with us awhile."

"Okay, Cookie, let's go see Dr. Sadie and get you on the mend." Frankie lovingly scooped up the sleeping cat who barely acknowledged being shoved into the crate.

"Cookie?" Carmen wondered.

Frankie laughed. "Well, the only thing this kitty has eaten is some warm milk and all the cookie crumbs off the kitchen floor. Until we know better, I guess that's her name."

Heading out the back door, crate in hand, Frankie noticed the lid was still askew on the forgotten birdseed bucket. "Shoot, poor birds. I forgot about you guys." Frankie drew her brows together though when she saw the seed container, now empty, sitting next to the large storage container on the porch. "Hmm, guess some lucky critter got a free meal," she mused, but her mouth dropped open when she saw the full feeders in the backyard. Giving silent thanks for her priceless business partner, Frankie set the container inside the bucket and closed the lid tightly, then loaded Cookie into Carmen's van, which was still warm.

As luck would have it, Sadie was having a quiet day, after a postponed surgery on a black lab from Pike Junction, about 20 miles north of Deep Lakes off Highway 76. Pike Junction received even more snow than Deep Lakes, and the owner wasn't in a hurry to drive the unplowed country roads.

Sadie cheerfully accepted the large slice of cherry kringle Frankie brought along as an offering. "Yum, cherry. That's going to go great with my morning coffee break. So, who did you bring me?"

Frankie relayed the story of finding the frozen feline, wondering if she was chipped for identification.

First, Sadie took the cat's temperature, then scanned her for a chip but shook her head sadly. "This little beauty is a young Norweigian Forest Cat. I'd say she's around three or four months old, tops, probably someone's new pet. She doesn't look like a street cat."

As Sadie spoke, she placed the kitten into a warming area, snuggled inside a blanket. Then the vet produced a hot water bottle from a warmer, and gently placed it underneath the blanket.

Frankie's sad eyes looked upon the sleeping kitty. "Is she going to be okay?"

"I should think so. Her temperature is borderline hypothermia, but she's warming up. I wonder how long she was outside and how she came to be there," Sadie said. "I'm going to keep her here for today, so I can monitor her. If nobody comes looking for her, I'll call you tomorrow to pick her up."

Back at the shop, Carmen, Jovie, Chloe and Sharmaine were working in cadence, but looked up expectantly at Frankie as she came through the door empty-handed.

"Dios Mío, Frankie," Carmen exclaimed, "don't tell me that poor little thing isn't okay!"

Frankie patted Carmen's floured hand. "Dr. Sadie wants to keep her until tomorrow. She's warming her up the right way to bring her temp back to normal."

Reassured, the women presented progress reports to

Frankie, who passed out compliments, genuinely relieved to have such competent bakers on hand. Carmen smiled warmly, also grateful.

Jovie had arrived, and every baker had sampled Frankie's coal lump cookies with tremendous satisfaction. Of course, each had their favorite lumps, so Frankie decided she'd bake several varieties and see what the customers liked best.

The business partners hoped to start decorating the shop windows that afternoon, so the remainder of the morning was filled with beaver-like industry as everyone baked, iced, and decorated cookies to the final stages, ready for the bakery case tomorrow.

Precisely at 1 p.m., Peggy Champagne rapped on the shop's front door, looking swanky in a long dark green peacoat with faux tortoise-shell buttons and black leather zip boots that wouldn't pass muster in deep snow. Peggy's shoulder-length white hair was the color of fresh snow and sparkling silver. Frankie opened the door and took the large tub her mother was carrying.

"Glad you're here, Mom. We're about to start organizing decorations." Gesturing at the tub, she added, "So, what's this?"

Peggy hung her long coat on the rack by the door and pulled off her boots, simultaneously fishing house slippers out of her oversized designer purse. Peggy was sophisticated but not in a snobby way and consummately prepared for every occasion. Knowing she would be up to her neck in dusty Christmas fare, Peggy wore blue jeans, a short-sleeved tee with an unbuttoned chambray shirt over the top, and still managed to look flawless.

Looking at her apron spackled with a variety of cookie batter dusted with flour clumps, Frankie often wondered how she came to be this maven's daughter.

The self-determined Peggy looked at the tub, remarking, "I was shopping at Shamrock Floral and The Hobby Hut for anything Victorian-looking and picked up some extra items for your windows, Dear."

Of course, you did, thought Frankie, bringing a sharp buzz in her ear from The Golden One. But truthfully, Frankie couldn't be more grateful. "Peggy Champagne saves the day again! Thank you, Mom."

The Bubble and Bake squad began opening boxes and bins, sorting decorations into piles that complied with the Victorian theme and laying aside others that did not. They worked long into the afternoon and into an early December darkness. At this point, Frankie cursed owning a corner store, with windows facing both Granite and Meriwether streets spanning some 40 feet or more. It was clear there wouldn't be enough Victorian to go around.

Pausing to assess their progress and make another list of necessary ornaments, the team was optimistic.

"There's plenty of lights and pine bough garland to fill the windows," Carmen noted.

Frankie nodded. "Mom, your angels and snowflakes are perfect, and so are the velvet birds—we just need more."

The cloth angels were made from eyelet with gold threads running throughout. The pearlescent white snowflakes glittered with simulated snow and shone in the soft glow of twinkle lights, while the red velvet cardinals flew about the plush pine boughs in a merry dance.

Peggy frowned slightly. "I'm afraid I bought all there was, Frankie. I don't know where you're going to find more in the next two days, Dear."

While Frankie was thinking of scoping out options online, Chloe volunteered to check the chain hobby store in Madison the next morning, before heading up to Deep Lakes. For now, work must stop and eating commence, so the crew donned winter garb and walked the few blocks to The Mud Puppy, a local bar and grill that was open year-round. Owner Kerby Hahn was happy for the business during the winter lull.

Never overlooking an opportunity, Frankie asked Kerby and his sister, Steffie, their server, which Christmas project they would like to sign on for this year. Steffie's eyes lit up—clearly she was on board with helping, but Kerby wasn't too sure. "The Mud Puppy isn't a chamber business, Frankie. We belong to the county Tavern League."

Frankie was nonplussed. "You're a downtown Deep Lakes business, so that shouldn't matter, Kerby. Anyway, there aren't any chamber officers stepping up for me to ask, and since they decided I should take charge… well, I say you're in. We could use someone to help with the ice rink plans."

Again, Steffie looked eager to join in, but Kerby was hesitant, pausing to give Frankie an even look as he wiped a couple of bar glasses. "Okay, I guess helping with the rink can't be too hard, right?" Kerby ventured.

Steffie brightened, nodding her agreement. Frankie pulled out her phone to add their names to her notes for later, taking down both of their cell numbers. "I'll let whoever's in charge of the committee know that you two are on board to help." Frankie smiled warmly at them, purposely omitting Bonnie Fleisner's name as committee chair.

Kerby's frown was obvious. "What do you mean 'whoever's in charge,' Frankie? You don't know who's in charge?"

Frankie leaned toward Kerby, speaking confidently. "No, not exactly. But, I'll know tomorrow! Keep you posted!" Frankie slapped a few dollars on the bar for a tip, slid off the high stool, and led the Bubble and Bake crew out the door.

The comforting bar food and calm night created a cheery atmosphere as they paraded back toward the bakery. Peggy chuckled softly and couldn't resist throwing a comment at Frankie. "That's my daughter, all right. You took on the town celebration without knowing what you're getting into."

Frankie wasn't sure where her mother's comments were heading, but she resisted the urge to protest, waiting her out.

"No matter what you do, Frankie, things always turn out just fine, so I'm not worried. It's just unfortunate that some of the town leaders aren't here to help you out. Doesn't seem very fair to me." Peggy was still protective of her only daughter.

"Never mind fairness. The fact is, someone had to step up to run the show, and I was nominated, for better or worse. So, as I always say, it will all happen because it has to happen," Frankie said, cheerfully.

Changing the subject, Frankie continued, "Okay, Mom, come clean. What kind of Victorian music can we expect at the tree lighting ceremony?"

"Oh, the traditional old Christmas carols, of course, like 'O Christmas Tree,' 'What Child Is This?' and 'Silent Night.' And the ensemble will work out a couple of lesser-known tunes as well. The real trick is finding people who play stringed instruments, you know." Peggy's brow was furled, but Chloe and Sharmaine looked excited.

"I think we can find you some people. My little brother is part of the Capital Youth Orchestra. They usually divide themselves up for holiday entertainment, and I think you can book them for a nominal fee," Sharmaine said, hoping to help.

Peggy was delighted. "Please give me their information as soon as we get back to the shop, and thanks a million, Sharmaine." Peggy was thrilled at the prospect of making one contact instead of several.

Back at Bubble and Bake, the women surveyed the decorating once more, Frankie frowning at the empty spaces still needing to be filled. Carmen patted her partner's shoulder. "Never mind, Frankie. We have a plan. You and I will look online, and Chloe will check out the craft stores in the morning."

"Okay, I guess that will have to do for now. I'll see you bright and early tomorrow to run the shop, right?" Now that Chloe and Sharmaine would be arriving late, Frankie and Carmen would have to run the morning bakery traffic. Usually, Carmen arrived later on Wednesdays, her typical day for helping Ryan out with farm chores.

"Oh, yeah, right. Thanks for reminding me. Ryan will be fine without me, or I'll get up extra early to help him." Carmen was good-natured about the prospect, however.

Chapter Three

Another restless night brought Frankie downstairs to the Bubble and Bake kitchen before 4 a.m. The bright white lights glared at her as she squinted to read the bulk coffee labels and fill her fancy espresso machine with a dark Costa Rican roast. The whirring sound was music to her ears followed by the anticipated aroma of perkiness in a mug.

The coffee machine's chugging finish reminded Frankie of the strange sounds she'd heard during the night as she lay awake. A rumbling noise like a train had interrupted her rambling thoughts, and as she paused to listen intently, she swore a ghostly train whistle had echoed in the darkness. But, how could that be? The train tracks hadn't been operative in Deep Lakes since the 1980's; in fact, the train depot was turned into a Bed and Breakfast a few years ago. As far as Frankie knew, the nearest train tracks were some 20 miles away and couldn't be heard around Deep Lakes.

Frankie frosted the waiting bismarcks and danishes for the pastry case, then braided together the coffee cake dough from the cooler after filling each with cherry, cranberry or apricot mixtures. Good thing Frankie could practically make pastries in her sleep, because the darkness of another short day outside the shop windows made her feel groggy.

The smell of baking sweets rising out of the oven only added to Frankie's desire to curl up somewhere and try to sleep. But her restless mind had other plans, and so did other forces beyond her. She heard the front door shop bell jingle and wondered if she accidentally left it unlocked last night. Checking the kitchen clock, she saw it was a little before 6, and Carmen wouldn't be arriving until just before 6:30.

Frankie padded out front and came face to face with a real-life gnome. The diminutive woman was shorter than Frankie, who barely managed five feet herself. Dressed in red leggings and a sky-blue wool parka with laced up fur-trimmed boots, the sprightly woman greeted Frankie merrily.

"I hope I didn't scare you, but I saw your shop light on and was hoping I could get something to eat. Your shop smells sublime. What time do you open?"

Frankie was surprised and wondered where this tiny woman had come from so early in the morning. But Frankie was inclined to be helpful and friendly. "I'm still finishing up some kitchen work before I open, but I have some pastries ready. Let me get you something. Do you like coffee or hot chocolate?"

The woman took off her parka and sat at one of the front tables in the shop. Frankie spied two long blonde braids hanging like suspenders down the front of her festive red and green plaid turtleneck. Frankie dashed to the kitchen and brought back a cinnamon roll and apple danish, two items she figured would please most palates.

"Thank you. Coffee would be lovely, please. Hmm. These smell delightful." The woman bent over the plate, inhaling deeply as she closed her eyes. "I'm Jewel, by the way." She held out one plump hand to meet Frankie's. Frankie caught the scent of creamy eggnog as their hands met.

"I'm Frankie. Happy to meet you." Frankie quickly returned with a mug of coffee from the shop brewer that would soon be wheeled out for customers. "May I ask what brings you here so early?"

"Well, my husband and I have just come in from the train," Jewel began, then noticed Frankie's mouth fall open.

"But the train doesn't come through Deep Lakes, not in years!" Frankie couldn't believe what Jewel was saying.

"Well, you see, the tracks on the regular route ended up broken from the big snow storm further on down, so the conductor told us they opened up the tracks here and we'd be stopping in Deep Lakes for a spell." Jewel took a bite of the danish and smiled approvingly.

"I see. Where is your husband then?" Frankie asked, marveling at Jewel's apparel and manner of speaking. She could imagine hearing her grandmother use the phrase "for a spell," but . . .

"Oh, we arrived in the middle of the night, so we took a room at the Depot B and B. Forrest was tuckered out after unloading our luggage, so he's still sleeping. But, I'm sure he'll be around later. He's got a terrible sweet tooth."

Frankie excused herself to the kitchen, telling Jewel to take as much time as she wished and to let Frankie know if she needed anything else. But minutes later, Frankie heard the bell jingle again, and when she went out front, Jewel was gone.

Lifting the mug and plate from the table, Frankie found three folded dollars. The last dollar had a peppermint-striped business card inside. The card read: Jewel and Forrest. Holiday Surprises of All Kinds. Text us: 1225.

Frankie looked at the back of the card for more information but found none. She wondered how useful the four-digit number would be, but stuck the card into her apron pocket as Carmen came through the back door.

"Hey, Carmen. You didn't see a little gnome lady on your way in, did you?" Frankie giggled at the look on Carmen's face.

"You haven't been getting enough sleep again, have you Frankie? What are you talking about—a gnome lady?" Carmen spoke with a hair band between her teeth as she donned a clean apron.

Frankie filled in Carmen, including the fact that she'd heard the train coming into town in the middle of the night, then showed her the business card Jewel had left on the table. Carmen looked skeptical.

"Things are getting a little weird around here. Figures she'd show up in our shop, Frankie." Frankie just laughed at Carmen's comment but had to admit that Bubble and Bake often seemed to be the vortex of quirky happenings, or perhaps Frankie herself was the magnetic center.

Carmen waited on bakery customers while Frankie sorted cookie orders by date. Some of the county organizations and businesses placed orders for their annual Christmas parties, as did several residents who were entertaining guests for the holidays. The December 9th cut-off date for ordering was rapidly approaching, but already, the shop had almost as many advance orders as the four bakers could handle. How lucky they were to have Sharmaine as part of their team.

Frankie had mixed up an industrial-sized batch of cut-out cookie dough and was prepping Molasses Crinkles when Carmen rolled into the kitchen, pushing the empty pastry case. Surprised at how quickly time was flying, Frankie noticed the clock read 8:45 a.m.

"We sold out. Seems like everyone in town is talking about another big snow storm coming our way," Carmen shook her head in disbelief. It was uncommon for the bakery to sell out completely, and to sell out early was even more unusual.

But, both women knew that in Wisconsin, the whiff of an impending snowstorm sent people flocking to stores to stock up, "just in case." Frankie suggested with a giggle, "I guess Bubble and Bake treats have now become a necessity!"

"That's okay by me," Carmen laughed, as she pulled out ingredients for spritz cookies.

Any variety of cookie that kept well in the freezer was being prepped in advance for shop orders. Most would be decorated into the wee hours of the morning the day before pick-up. Frankie and Carmen rolled out, scooped, and molded cookie dough accompanied by happy Christmas tunes on the local radio station.

A productive morning was in full swing when Frankie's phone rang with Dr. Sadie on the line. "Your Norweigian Forest Cat looks good as new this morning. Nobody has contacted the office, so you can pick her up if you still want to host her as a shop visitor." Frankie agreed, letting Sadie know she would pick the lost kitty up around lunch time.

Minutes later, Chloe and Sharmaine opened the back door, looking doleful. Chloe was carrying a small bag from a craft store, certainly not large enough to contain many shop decorations.

Opening the bag, Chloe pulled out a few painted wooden doves with gold accents. "This was all I could find in the two stores we stopped at this morning. Either Victorian decorations aren't a thing this year or they're a big thing, because there aren't any to be found."

Frankie and Carmen exchanged looks of frustration,

but Frankie reassured Chloe. "It's okay. We'll just have to make do. Maybe we can spread out the ornaments we have and add more lights. Lights are pretty easy to come by. Meanwhile, we have lots of baking and prep work, so let's get to it." The rhythm of work returned to the kitchen as well as the occasional singing of carols.

At lunch time, Frankie dashed out the back door where her trusty blue SUV was parked on the concrete slab behind the shop. Standing on the snow-covered creek trail, she saw Jewel tossing birdseed to the ground feeders. Frankie smiled at the array of feathered friends clamoring for seeds: juncos, grosbeaks, red polls, finches and at least six bright red male cardinals pecked around for sunflower seeds.

"If only I could borrow you for my shop windows," Frankie said, causing Jewel to turn around to look.

"Whatever do you mean, Frankie?" Jewel asked.

Frankie explained the Victorian theme for this year's Christmas celebration, noting the shop only had about half as many ornaments as they needed to finish the decorating.

Jewel's face brightened, her cheeks two tiny plump apples. "I think I might be able to help you. Forrest and I were on our way to the Norske Jul fair in Iola before we got waylaid by the train. I have all kinds of handmade ornaments that just might work for your shop!"

Frankie looked at the pint-sized woman and clapped her hands. "Oh Jewel, if that's true, please go get them, and we'll all take a look as soon as I get back from the vet. I have to pick up a kitty." Frankie fairly skipped to the SUV.

At Dr. Sadie's, Cookie Cat seemed pleased to see her rescuer again, purring loudly at Frankie and rubbing her head repeatedly on Frankie's ankles. Sadie promised to keep Frankie informed of any calls to her office inquiring about the feline. On the way back to Bubble and Bake, Ted Lennon called from public works.

"Hi Frankie. Any luck getting those decorations out of storage, yet?" Ted wondered.

"Oh shoot, Ted," Frankie knew she was supposed to be doing something else that morning. "I'm afraid I haven't rounded up any bodies yet. Did you get the plumbing fixed at City Hall?"

Ted confirmed the plumbing was in working order. "So, I have some time if you can find a few helpers. I can meet you out at the highway department this afternoon. Might be your best window of opportunity, if ya know what I'm saying. Looks like we're in for another storm, and that could put the kibosh on getting at the decorations."

Frankie knew not to look a gift horse in the mouth. She could use Ted's help and his truck, so she agreed to find some people and meet him later that afternoon before dark.

Back at the bakery, Cookie Cat settled nicely into a sunny spot in the wine lounge, and Frankie filled in the crew about Jewel's upcoming visit with handmade ornaments.

Carmen's eyes couldn't stop themselves from twinkling. "Oh boy, we get to meet the mysterious gnome lady." But when Jewel danced into the store, Carmen's eyes popped, taking in the little lady with braids the color of custard who smelled like holiday eggnog.

Nobody in the shop seemed to notice that Cookie Cat sniffed the air when Jewel came in the door, then disappeared in a flash to hide in the office under the desk.

Introductions were made, and Jewel opened painted Christmas boxes revealing an array of ornaments perfect for the Victorian theme. Laid out on the walnut bar, the women exclaimed over and over as they picked up different ones, admiring the birds and angels made from delicate lace, some embroidered with silver or gold threads. They chose a number of red lace cardinals, angels whose skirts were dotted with clear gems, and pearlescent snowflakes in several designs.

Jewel was pleased to help and offered them a bargain price for the assortment, but Carmen interjected as Frankie waved her hand, shaking her head, too.

"Uh-uh, no way, Jewel. You saved us, and we're paying you full price," Carmen said with a big smile.

Frankie agreed and let out a sigh of relief that at least one thing was almost accomplished on the Christmas task list. Then she remembered her call with Ted Lennon.

"Okay, everyone, listen up. I have to find volunteers to go out to the city storage and help load up the decorations to go to Spurgeon Park. Ted from public works says we have to do it today because he has time, the keys, and a truck. Any ideas who might help?"

It was agreed that Chloe and Sharmaine should finalize shop decorating, but Carmen said she'd call her twins, Kyle and Carlos, to meet them at the storage to help.

"It's not until after school, and I'll let Ryan know they'll be home a little late for chores today," Carmen volunteered.

Frankie, too, had a brainstorm to call her brother, Nick, a floor supervisor at Triple Crown Marine, Whitman County's foremost employer and maker of inboard and outboard boat motors. Nick was always willing to do physical labor for Frankie, help out with wine bottling, and tote cases of wine to Frankie's basement by the hundreds. And, Nick was popular, not just as a ladies' man, but he also had a large circle of friends and poker buddies, many who owed him favors. Frankie hoped to capitalize on Nick's popularity today.

Promptly at 4 p.m., a convergence of locals and Jewel waited outside city storage on County HH and 4th Avenue, a couple miles east of town. Frankie wondered if Jewel walked to the storage garage, and how she knew where to find it. She also looked around for her husband but didn't see anyone who fit the bill.

Ted pulled up in the orange city truck, blending in perfectly with the blaze orange highway plows, which were parked face out, ready to sally forth into the next snow event. Ted laughed as he hauled his large frame out of the pick-up, surveying the group.

"Well, Frankie, looks like ya did alright rounding up people." Ted had a jovial manner and found even the most commonplace things humorous. "Let me fish out my keys here…" As Ted walked toward a large pole building with a triple overhanging door, an enormous loop of keys announced themselves with a noisy jangle.

"You know, I seldom go into this particular shed, so I'm not sure which key to use here." Frankie and the others watched Ted as he appeared to study each key in the waning daylight. Carmen's sons, Carlos and Kyle, were amused, but impatient, watching Ted. Frankie's brother, Nick, offered his assistance, and Ted was appreciative. "My eyes aren't as good as they once were, and my fingers are pretty stiff these days, too," Ted ventured, handing the large key ring to Nick.

Nick tried key after key, adeptly, but with no success. Inside Frankie's brain, a storm was spitting up sparks of fire. Why couldn't anything just be simple, she wondered, and a taunting laugh echoed somewhere inside her mind from The Golden One in reply. Inertia was difficult for Frankie, and she desperately wanted to snatch the keys and try them herself, but knew she wouldn't be able to go any faster than Nick was already. So, she stood there stamping her feet to stay warm, watching her breath billow out into the cold air.

Finally, Nick pronounced he had tried every key,

some of them twice, and asked Ted if there was another set of keys somewhere they might try. Frankie gave her patient brother a lot of credit for not giving up. In that moment, she loved him dearly. Nick could be anywhere else, but he was here, offering his little sister help only because she had asked.

A small gloved hand reached out to grab Nick's arm gently. It was Jewel, looking like a robust pixie in the half-light. "Here, let me have a go at it. I'm very good at unlocking things," Jewel said softly, taking the keys effortlessly from Nick's hand.

Nick scoffed a bit, but was amused by Jewel. As he stepped aside, Jewel had the overhead door lock undone in no time at all. Nick's jaw dropped as he examined the large antique-looking key inside the lock mechanism. "I didn't even see this key," he said, "I don't know how I could have missed it."

Thankfully, Ted had the notion to pull the pick-up close to the entry, shining its headlights into the storage area so the decorations could be found. Thank goodness Adele hadn't been creative with the labels, simply marking them "Christmas Decorations."

In no time the boxes were loaded onto the city truck and hauled to Spurgeon Park. Frankie noticed that Jewel was no longer with the group and wondered how she managed to come and go, seemingly in the blink of an eye.

The decorations were stacked under the gazebo until decorating could commence, a thought that made Frankie chew her bottom lip, wondering when exactly decorating would begin, and furthermore, who would be doing it? Her stomach turned a little somersault as The Golden One simultaneously began nagging her to find people to take charge of the various Christmas festival projects.

"Goldie's right, Cherie; you cannot do this yourself, and the sooner you delegate, the better," Pirate spoke soothingly from Frankie's shoulder.

Frankie invited anyone who was willing to come back to Bubble and Bake to finish decorating, promising baked goods, pizzas, and beverages. She knew Chloe and Sharmaine were capable, but she felt guilty about leaving the entire task to them.

Nick gave Frankie a tight hug but declined. "I'm shooting pool tonight at The Mud Puppy with some work guys. Sorry, Sis." Frankie gave him the ok sign and her thanks.

Carmen and Frankie were on their own for the evening, as the twins needed to book it home to help their dad feed sheep and dogs.

From Granite Street's front, Bubble and Bake was aglow with white lights, illuminating the shop windows and reflecting off the bejeweled doves, snowflakes and angels. The effect was dazzling. Chloe and Sharmaine had left their bosses a note and were on their way back to Madison. Carmen and Frankie hugged as tears came to Frankie's eyes.

"It looks amazing. I'm so thankful to have one item

crossed off the list," Frankie's voice faltered. Instead of enjoying the completed decorations, Frankie's insides were a stew of worry. She wondered if this Christmas would be just like the others—lacking perfection.

"Oh, Carmie, I think I bit off too big a bite this time. I have no idea how to make this work without calling every business owner in town."

Carmen had great faith in Frankie, however, and told her so. As long as the two had known each other, since elementary school, Frankie was always diving impulsively into big projects, but never once failed to see them through. "Things will work out, Frankie. I'll help you tomorrow. Let it rest for now," Carmen said.

"Thanks, Carmie. You head home to your family, and I'll see you bright and early tomorrow," Frankie pretended good humor but didn't perk up much, thinking the night was still young—she ought to be able to accomplish something.

With Carmen out the door, Frankie dragged out her list of Christmas festival tasks and decided she better see Bonnie Fleisner tomorrow morning at the hardware store. *I can't avoid her forever, after all, and I need to cross the ice rink project off my list,* Frankie thought, remembering she had planned to see Bonnie yesterday.

The ice rink area at Spurgeon Park was the designated gathering spot after the tree lighting ceremony took place at the gazebo. Ice sculptors from all over arrived two days before the ceremony to carve giant ice blocks that surrounded the rink. After the tree lighting and Victorian music performance, the crowd would gather at the rink where the sculptures were unveiled with fanfare. Visitors voted for their favorites in several categories, then indulged in hot cocoa, mulled cider, roasted nuts and savory chili while the votes were tallied, followed by awards and trophies.

The ice sculptures were one of the many highlights of Deep Lakes Christmases for years. Frankie smiled at the memory of her daughters, Sophie and Violet, arguing over which sculpture was best, sipping hot cocoa, bundled up in parkas, scarves wound around them so thick the only things visible were their tiny red noses and gleaming eyes. Somewhere in time, the girls transitioned from discussing sculptures to chatting about which town boy they hoped would show up to buy them cocoa or cider.

Now, Sophie was a young woman, working as a nurse in Madison, living with Max, another nurse she'd met at the hospital. Violet was a sophomore at UW-Stevens Point, tottering back and forth among various majors, uncertain about her path. Frankie wondered how they grew up so quickly, how time had seemed to get away from her.

"And that's precisely the reason you should spend more time with your mother, Francine," Goldie chided, and Frankie knew better than to argue with that voice.

As if on cue, the shop door opened, revealing Peggy Champagne, bags in tow. Frankie marveled that her mother never arrived any place empty-handed.

Breathless, Peggy plunked down a white restaurant bag on the counter next to Frankie. "I imagine you haven't eaten dinner, so I brought you something from Sterling Creek. Broasted chicken, coleslaw, and a baked potato with sour cream."

Frankie's stomach growled in anticipation. Sterling Creek Supper Club was a year-round business frequented by locals since 1955, originally owned by Leon and Joan Zinski, then passed down to their sons, Ed and Jerry, who with their wives, were serving up broasted chicken, pork chops, prime rib, and famous fish fry fare.

"You're wonderful, Mother," Frankie said, squeezing Peggy's shoulder. "And you're right, as usual. I'm trying to work on this list."

Peggy brightened, held up one finger, and dug a piece of paper from her handbag. "Oh yes, your list. I have something that might help you. Here."

The paper was a list of committee members' names and contact information from last year's Christmas celebration. Frankie couldn't contain herself. "Where in the world did you get this?"

Peggy shrugged, conveying her own puzzlement. "Funny thing. The historical society met tonight at the supper club to finalize the music for the tree lighting ceremony. When I gathered up my notes, this piece of paper was stuck underneath my notebook."

Frankie turned over the paper, inspected it, and found something sticky. She lifted it to her nose, concluded that honey or maybe jelly had served its purpose as a glue, but that didn't explain how it happened to show up at the supper club. No matter—the list in hand renewed her spirits and determination.

Pulling a bottle of Hygge Holiday from the wine fridge behind the bar, Frankie poured her mother and herself a small portion, and raised her glass in salute to Peggy, who had surely saved the day again. And just in time, because outside, Deep Lakes was a sitting duck for another snow storm.

Chapter Four

Promptly at 6 a.m., Jewel knocked on the back door of Bubble and Bake, seeking early admittance for coffee and kringle. Frankie smiled brightly as Jewel stamped her snowy boots on the back deck, then left them outside as she pulled a pair of blue velvet house slippers from a tote bag. Jewel's hair was wound up in a braided bun at the nape of her neck, just visible under her red cap that looked like a Poinsettia blossom with flocked snow clusters.

Frankie suggested Jewel sit at the kitchen counter while she finished loading the bakery case for the morning. "Sorry about the weather, Jewel. Looks like you might be stuck in Deep Lakes a little longer."

"Oh, by the way, you have to meet our orphaned kitty. I think you'll like her." Frankie sidestepped the rug where Cookie Cat had been curled into a ball next to the heat vent, but the cat was nowhere to be seen. "Huh, well never mind. You can meet her later."

As Jewel savored a Bavarian cream kringle wedge, Frankie explained her plans to get in touch with the Christmas committee people, now that she had last year's list, a miraculous gift from her mother.

"If only you could gather them all together at once, that would save so much time, Frankie," Jewel offered. The small woman gave Frankie a sideways glance, then pretended to study her pastry.

A brainstorm erupted, and Frankie clapped and gave Jewel a hug. "You're a genius, Jewel! I can get them all together, right here. Tonight, after the store windows are judged. Every business owner should be around for the judging!"

Frankie allowed a giddy giggle to escape. "This is perfect, Jewel. I can have them here for a planning party. They can all talk to each other at once and get their plans made. In fact, I'm going to call the city clerk and offer to have the awards given out right here! That will save everyone time."

Jewel smiled secretively, hopped off the stool, and began bundling up to leave. Frankie thanked her again, handed her a bakery bag with kringle wedges to take to Forrest, then checked the clock, wondering if all of her helpers would be late today due to the overnight snow.

The area TV weatherman reported Deep Lakes had the highest snow totals with nine inches of the white stuff. The country roads would be slow going for Carmen, and since Chloe and Sharmaine had an hour drive in good weather, today was sure to be challenging.

Frankie didn't have time to dawdle, in any case. She retrieved her office laptop and, armed with the list from her mom, crafted a group email, suggesting Bubble and

Bake as a meeting place for the decorating awards and after-meeting.

Just as Frankie flipped the switch on the open sign, Carmen arrived, smiling wider than normal.

"You're in a good mood this morning, Carmie. What's up?" Frankie asked her friend, who was unwinding her long woolen scarf and pulling off thermal gloves.

Carmen pointed out the front shop windows along Granite Street, and Frankie almost cried to see Carlos and Kyle pushing snow shovels up the sidewalk as if they were in a race to see who could finish first.

"School's closed today. Too much snow, and it didn't stop until almost 5 this morning. So, we did chores, and I brought them here to help." Carmen looked pleased with herself. "Of course, we'll have to pay them in kringle!" She laughed heartily. "Your turn, Frankie. You look about to burst, so you must have some good news?"

Frankie recounted her mother coming to the shop with the list of committee contacts and added Jewel's idea of getting everyone together in one place to plan.

"The little gnome lady strikes again," Carmen said mischievously. Frankie gave Carmen a fist bump.

With few morning customers, the bakery case squeaked back to the kitchen, looking ready for a party. "Oh well, looks like tomorrow is discount day," Frankie proclaimed. "That's okay. It will give us time to bake for cookie orders, plus I need to make gingerbread for the gingerbread house contest."

Carmen bagged up some of the morning leftovers for her sons to take back to the farm, warned them to take it easy on the road home, and stood on tiptoe to peck each one on the cheek. Carmen was a few inches taller than the vertically challenged Frankie, but Carlos and Kyle were nearly six feet and still growing.

The boys grimaced a little at Carmen's kisses, half-jokingly, and Frankie couldn't resist the opportunity to make them cringe a bit more. She headed their direction and grabbed each one for a hug around the waist. "Thank you both so much for shoveling us out today," she gushed intentionally. "You saved my aching back." The two regarded Frankie as if she were a matronly aunt they had to tolerate. Frankie laughed though, and so did the boys.

Carmen was batching peanut butter cookie dough when Chloe and Sharmaine arrived, reporting that the four-lanes had one lane plowed, but the rest of the highway into town was snow-covered, but manageable at a slow speed.

The two quickly went to work on more sugar cookie dough, and with the kitchen humming, Frankie excused herself to call the city clerk to offer Bubble and Bake for the awards ceremony that night. Miraculously, Kelley thought the idea was splendid, "much cozier than the bland city hall meeting room," she said. Kelley said she would call the judges and the newspaper, since Frankie took care of contacting the businesses.

How easy it had been to arrange the awards and meeting in such a short time. Frankie wondered if her next task would go just as smoothly. She slid pieces of apple cinnamon and almond kringle onto a plate and into a waxed bakery bag as a friendly offering to Bonnie Fleisner.

Fleisner's Hardware had seen better days. An old-fashioned downtown hardware store, the small piece of real estate could barely compete against the giant warehouse-sized chains off Riverside Parkway on the north end of town. Besides the usual tools, plumbing and electrical whatnot, Fleisner's had a small selection of camping and fishing gear, bird feeders and seed, and seasonal supplies. The garden hoses and lawn chairs of summer had been replaced by snow shovels and sidewalk salt. It was no secret that Bonnie wanted to sell the store and retire, but her husband held onto the family business, albeit with less enthusiasm each winter.

Bonnie was at the front register when Frankie entered, sounding off the electronic chime. Bonnie raised her head hopefully from the catalog she was studying. When she saw it was only Frankie, an unlikely customer, she scowled.

Frankie plastered an extra-cheerful expression on her face and extended her arm with the bakery bag. "Good morning, Bonnie. I brought you some kringle," Frankie began, hoping to break the ice with small talk.

"Hmph. What's so good about it? All this snow lately makes my back hurt. I keep telling Judd we could be sitting in Florida right now, soaking up the sunshine. Instead, here we are—stuck for another long winter."

Frankie didn't recall ever seeing Bonnie pick up a snow shovel. Judd always had the snow blower going early in the morning to clear the walk in front of the store. One perk of owning a hardware store must be a discount on things like mowers and blowers, Frankie imagined. Still, she noticed the two were cutting back here and there. The store seemed to carry less Christmas decorations each year, and less than half of the overhead lights were on in the store, making passersby wonder if it was even open for business.

Frankie resumed her lighthearted chatter. "Well, I bet you're selling lots of snow shovels and salt these days."

Bonnie produced a glower in response and snatched the bakery away from Frankie like a hungry mutt. "So, you buying anything today?" The question was Bonnie's reply to friendly chit-chat.

By the time Frankie headed back down the street to the shop, she was pushing a dolly with 25 pounds of bird seed, two heavy duty extension cords, and several sets of bubble lights that had surely been sitting around a decade at Fleisner's. But, she also left with a grudging agreement that Bonnie would be at the gathering of committee members that night.

"I don't see why I should take on Kerby and Steffie Hahn, though. They aren't part of the chamber, and they have no Christmas festival experience," Bonnie huffed.

By now, Frankie was finished with pleasantries. She figured she'd already purchased enough from Bonnie to get something in exchange without any more guff. "Well, as my mother always told me, many hands make light work. The Hahns want to help, so they should. See you later."

Crossing the bridge on Meriwether Street over Sterling Creek, Frankie was distracted by a bobbing red triangle, the same pointy red bobber she swore she saw the other day before Cookie Cat showed up in her alley. Now, however, the pointy red hat was replaced by another diversion: a medium-sized dog romped along the creek, barking at the trunk of a tree behind Frankie's shop.

"What next?" Frankie said aloud, rolling the dolly as fast as the wheels would turn, around the corner, and down the alley. She pulled up to the shop's back steps and parked the dolly, and peered at the fluffy black and gray dog that had proudly treed one of the neighborhood squirrels.

The hound turned in Frankie's direction, clearly happy to see a new playmate and bounded head-on toward her. Frankie pushed the dolly in front of her in case the dog was an unfriendly beast, but he sat down in the snow at her feet, promptly rolled onto his back and offered his tummy, hopeful of a rubdown. Frankie laughed and knelt down slowly, offering her hand for a sniff, then gently patted the dog's head, neck and stomach.

The fluffy dog had no collar or harness, and its long pink tongue hung out, clearly in need of a drink. As if reading

Frankie's thoughts, the dog turned over and scooped up a couple mouthfuls of snow, then sat down obediently at her feet again. Frankie looked in both directions as far as the eye could see, but nobody was in sight.

"Okay, I guess I'm supposed to take care of you, too," Frankie said aloud to the dog, who barked and nodded its head, as if understanding her words. "Come on. Let's get you up to the deck."

The hound followed Frankie up the steps as Frankie took inventory of its condition. It must have been outside playing for awhile, as balls of snow hung like a fringe of pom-poms from its thick, coarse fur. Of course, the dog was thirsty and seemed to be ready for a nap. Who knows how far it had run that morning? Frankie wondered if the pooch had followed the creek bed or maybe even had come from further up the river. She planned to call Dr. Sadie, hoping her second animal foundling this week had a chip.

Chloe poked her head out the back door to see what the ruckus was all about, grinning at the dog and laughing at Frankie. "You sure do seem to attract critters, Frankie Champagne," Chloe remarked. "What can I do to help?"

Together, the women barricaded the hound onto the deck by blocking the stairs with an upturned picnic table. Carmen fetched water and produced some dog jerky from her coat pocket, saying she always carried treats for the farm dogs. The grateful canine ate everything and was looking for more.

"Guess I'll take this furry friend over to Sadie's right now. She always has food on hand." Frankie recalled the dolly was still sitting by the steps. "Maybe someone can ride with me to help wrangle the dog, and someone else can unload the dolly and take it back to Fleisner's." Frankie shot Carmen a warning look. "Don't even ask. I'll tell you later."

Chloe, who seemed comfortably capable with dogs, hopped in the back of Frankie's SUV and the two sped off to Dr. Sadie's.

Sadie's eyes were wide seeing Frankie walk into her clinic the second time in a week, this time with a pooch, no less. Sadie was manning the reception area again today as the snow storm meant cancellations, and Sadie's receptionist was running late due to the roads.

"Just give me one second, and I'll grab a collar and leash from the back." Sadie was prepared for most animal emergencies, keeping a handy supply of extra accessories around.

Back in a flash, Sadie expertly snapped the collar loosely onto the hound and clipped on the leash, then led him to the scale, handing Frankie the clipboard marked "patient information."

Sadie's light curls bobbed as she petted the dog, who seemed to recognize her.

"Do you know this critter?" Frankie wondered.

Sadie shrugged. "Could be. Frankie, meet the Norwegian elkhound. Probably full grown." Sadie peered into the hound's mouth, examining and counting teeth. "And, by the way, *she's* not a male. She's 48 pounds, and that's about right for a full-grown female."

Sadie snapped a photo of her as she perched happily on the clinic scale. "If you have a minute, I'll scan her for a chip. If she's chipped, she can stay here while I contact the owner. If not…" Sadie let the question hang in the air as she met Frankie's eyes.

"Oh, sure, why not?" Frankie held up both hands. "Welcome to Bubble and Bake and Buddies," she laughed.

Sadie was back in a couple of minutes, holding a large bag of dog kibble. "Congratulations, Frankie, you're the temporary owner of an Elkie, that's the official term of endearment used by owners. And, if I'm not mistaken, this is the second Norwegian breed you've inherited in so many days," Sadie laughed, eyebrows raised.

Realization sunk in, making Frankie wonder if there was something to this or merely coincidence. Both animals showed up behind Bubble and Bake. Both were preceded by a red triangular bobbing thing that resembled a gnome hat.

Even more interesting was the phantom train showing up about the same time in Deep Lakes with Jewel, who resembled every inch a Scandinavian nisse, which is the equivalent of a sprite or gnome. Well, to be fair, Jewel was taller than the nisser of folklore, but she was short just the same, maybe just four and a half feet, by Frankie's guesstimate.

Every creature surrounding Bubble and Bake this week pointed to Scandinavia. Was someone taunting her, or had the legendary nisser come to play for the holidays? Frankie's business reflected her Danish heritage from the buttery kringle to the simple shop furniture, from her dad's whimsical carvings to the hygge atmosphere she cultivated with candles, essential oils, and comfy floor cushions. Was she supposed to believe her ancestors were intervening in her life?

Frankie's own sweet Grandma Sophie, a small, plump Danish woman, was responsible for her love of baking. Frankie's darling grandmother taught her how to make kringles and other pastries, rolling dough, singing songs, and telling folktales to Frankie in her kitchen. Frankie found it hard to believe that her own mother was Sophie's daughter—the two had nothing in common from their looks to their likes. Was Grandma Sophie trying to send her a message? If so, what in the world was she supposed to take from the messengers: a cat, a dog and a nisse-lady?

The golden-eyed elkhound nuzzled Frankie's hand with her soft muzzle, hunched down in submission, and made a quiet woof, as if answering her inner questions, making it known the two were meant to be together for some reason.

"Yes, you're coming home with me," Frankie cooed, stroking her velvety ears. Where were Frankie's dependable fireflies right now, she queried to herself. She expected The Golden One to admonish her, first for taking in the elkhound, secondly, for entertaining the possibility of the intervention of magical creatures. But, since Jewel arrived in Deep Lakes, The Golden One seemed to have flown south for the winter. Frankie laughed at her own joke, and when her eyes met the elkhound's, she was smiling secretly at her temporary master.

Chapter Five

"Guess I'll call you Elkie for now," Frankie said quietly, setting an old woven rag rug in the small alcove between the kitchen and wine lounge she used as a business office. "I wish I knew if you were used to being indoors or around other people or what?"

Elkie lifted her head toward Frankie's questions, drew her brows together and nodded. "Okay, so which of those questions are you answering in the affirmative?" Frankie often talked to herself, so she was happy for a flesh and blood companion to make her feel more normal. Especially right now, when she was alone in the shop since Carmen and Jovie had left to run personal errands, and Chloe and Sharmaine were on their way back to Madison. The interns would be logging plenty of extra hours and coming in early tomorrow.

She headed out to the kitchen, where sheets of gingerbread filled the ovens, to retrieve dishes of chow and water for Elkie, when she heard a ruckus. Clattering toenails on the hardwood floors, barking, and demonic yowling surged through the walls, followed by a crash. The noise came from the wine lounge. Frankie envisioned the shop Christmas tree toppled over, ornaments shattered on the floor.

The chow forgotten, Frankie hurried to the lounge as a silver streak passed her and dived into the kitchen before the door swung shut again. Well, at least one animal was out of the danger zone for now. The tree was lying on its side as expected. Elkie stood over the tree like a witness at a crime scene, barking loudly, clearly implicating Cookie as the culprit of the incident. Frankie laughed in spite of the situation, then skirted around the tree to assess the damages. Miraculously, the china ice skater, a keepsake from her father, was still attached to its pine branch, unscathed. This was the second time the ice skater had survived tragedy.

The first time was in the house fire five years ago where Frankie lost most of her belongings. She remembered the daunting task of opening damaged containers, some soot-covered, some wet from fire hoses. She dreaded looking through their belongings; it made her feel like a victim each time she opened a new box or drawer.

The reminder of the house fire made Frankie pause momentarily. Was the fire the third strike in Frankie's life that fizzled her Christmas spirit beyond repair? Could that be another reason Frankie stayed busy—the urge to control something in her life after facing the uncontrollable? Had she even faced the uncontrollable or just swept it under the rug?

She allowed the rest of the memory to play back in her mind. When she opened the Christmas container there was the treasured skater, surrounded by melted plastic, but completely intact, only needing a scrub to take off the sooty residue. Frankie had lovingly placed her on a windowsill to air out the smoky smell of the fire. Now, the skater looked serenely up at Frankie, as if being tipped over was a common occurrence.

The porcelain angel atop the tree didn't fare quite as well. Obviously, the angel bore the brunt of the tree's free fall. It had been decapitated and suffered a broken foot as well. Frankie crouched on her stomach, peering around for the head as Elkie pounced on Frankie's bottom, enjoying this new game. Locating the angel's head underneath the two-piece sofa, Frankie managed to grab it and right herself before Elkie pounced again.

Frankie waggled one finger at the hound. "You cannot be running around the shop like a banshee," she scolded. Holding the angel's head aloft, she added, "Just look what you've done, Elkie!" Elkie managed to look contrite while Frankie held her collar and firmly led her back to the office area.

Now it was time to find that Cookie Cat and give her a scolding as well. Frankie opened the kitchen door and was greeted by the spicy scent of baking gingerbread.

"My gingerbread, argh!" Frankie knew her effort to keep up with the holiday baking was down the drain for today. As if verifying her discovery, the timer chimed again, Frankie guessed for probably the fiftieth time, and announced the ruin of the gingerbread. But, when she opened the first oven doors, the gingerbread was perfectly browned. All the subsequent cookie sheets were in accord with the first. Frankie's eyes darted about the kitchen, looking for tiny sprites or maybe a fluttering angel. "I don't know what's going on around here, but thank you—whomever."

She spied Cookie Cat wedged into a space behind her spice cabinet, just a pair of golden eyes glowing in the shadows. "And you, Cookie, can forget about gingerbread crumbs for today. I'm taking you upstairs for the rest of the afternoon, so I can get my work done in peace." She bent down, scooted the cat out of the nook, brushed a cobweb from one ear and carried her upstairs, depositing her in the kitchen next to a dish of kitty food, conveniently located near a heat vent.

Frankie resumed baking, sporadically checking her emails until she was satisfied she'd received mostly positive responses to her invitation to attend the planning meeting after the awards.

Mentally checking off items in her head, Frankie decided she needed to step up quiche preparation for what would certainly be a busy weekend for the wine lounge. Thankfully, Chloe had prepared all of the crusts, cut up veggies and shredded cheese, lightening Frankie's load.

Tomorrow's pastries were finished except for icing, which would be a morning chore. Chloe and Sharmaine planned to arrive by 5, and Carmen said she'd be there about the same time, so Frankie would bake the rest of the gingerbread that night—at least that was the plan.

This time of year, she wished the shop had extra hands, which reminded her she must talk to Jovie to see how many hours she could spare the rest of the week.

The day was getting away from her, and she still had to hightail it to church for a short choir ensemble practice. Steve the director had called earlier to suggest squeezing in an hour or so that afternoon. Gritting her teeth, Frankie agreed, wondering how she could add more minutes to the day.

Before heading out the back door, Frankie checked on her menagerie, finding both Cookie and Elkie snoozing away in the late afternoon lull: Cookie upstairs on Frankie's bed, and Elkie downstairs in the office. She paused to admire the shop's Christmas lights and the ambient vibe they created.

She frowned when she walked past her injured angel sitting on the bar, adding "repair angel" to her unending task list. She wondered how long she'd be playing hostess to the cat and dog, thinking their owners must be worried, missing them. Turning her face upwards, she whispered, "Deep Lakes sure could use a Christmas miracle, if You have time."

*   *   *

About an hour later, Frankie breezed through the back door, still humming "Angels We Have Heard On High," the last song from practice. The musical break rejuvenated her spirit, plus she had seen both Jovie and Carmen, who said they would meet her shortly at the shop to get ready for the awards and meeting.

Elkie let out a gruff bark alarm when Frankie arrived, so she called the dog into the kitchen, let her out the back door for business purposes, and gave her some loving strokes around the ears and neck. Elkie ate all the food Frankie left and drank most of the water, so she refilled her water dish, hoping the hound was ready to resume sleeping in the alcove.

But Elkie had other plans, running around in a circle from the alcove to the lounge area and back again, obviously wanting to play. Frankie mentally noted the dog would need a walk in the morning and planned an early alarm, exactly the opposite of the morning routine she'd set in her mind. Elkie was relentless.

"Okay, you win, Elkie. Let's see what Sadie sent along for toys." Frankie pulled out a squeaky rubber squirrel with a whirling tail and tossed it down the hallway. Elkie's ears perked up, her eyes brightened, and she dashed down the hallway, flew past the toy, and stood at the corner by the wine lounge entrance, nodding and woofing for Frankie to follow.

Shaking her head and muttering, Frankie reluctantly trudged to the waiting dog, who gestured with her head and wagging tail to keep following. Elkie stopped at the walnut wine bar and barked purposefully.

"Okay, what'll you have, Elkie? Beer, wine? I don't

have any doggy treats in here." Frankie looked at the dog, puzzled.

In response, Elkie stood on two legs, placed her front feet on the bar stool seat, produced an exaggerated nod toward the bar top, and barked again, more sharply.

"Seriously, Dog, I can't imagine what you want…" Frankie's voice trailed off abruptly when she noticed her angel was gone. Flipping the lights on behind the bar, she looked on the floor and underneath the bar stools, but no angel.

Now Frankie's temper flared. "Did you take the angel? Did you eat the angel? Oh, no." Frankie glared at Elkie, who managed a hurtful expression, even as she led Frankie to the corner of the room where the Christmas tree stood. Frankie had to look twice to comprehend that an angel was perched atop the tree, just as it should be. It certainly looked like Frankie's angel, but she couldn't be sure unless she retrieved the step ladder to examine the topper.

By now, the kitchen was clattering with activity, and Frankie heard Carmen's and Jovie's voices calling her name. A bewildered Frankie with the golden-eyed elkhound on her heels, trotted into the kitchen. Frankie wondered if she should even mention the angel, but knew she wore her feelings all over her face and couldn't get away with anything when Carmen was around.

"You and that dog both look like you just saw a ghost, Frankie. What's going on?" There was Carmen, right on cue.

"The broken angel topper I told you about. Well, it's magically fixed and back on top of our tree. Elkie took me to see it." Frankie still wasn't certain she could believe it.

"Well, maybe your mom came while you were at the church and fixed it to surprise you." Carmen would be the one to craft a practical reason, which Frankie found acceptable.

"Okay, well then, let's get busy. Divide and conquer?" Frankie and Carmen always looked at their list, tore it in the number of pieces to match the number of workers, and got on with it.

Jovie prepared flatbread pizzas and cut up the finished kringles into wedges, cleaning up her work station along the way. Frankie loved how Jovie managed to work with precision, almost floating through the kitchen tasks. Jovie commented on her mother's most recent ailments, which were lengthy and unusual. That was actually normal for Mrs. Luedtke, who relied on Jovie for years, beginning in middle school. Bubble and Bake and Shamrock Floral were respites for Jovie, who needed an outlet and listening ears.

Working like busy bees, Carmen and Frankie tackled Raspberry Snow Bars, Seven Layer Bars and Congo Bars for the judges of the window decorating contest. The identities of the judges were top secret, kept under wraps until after the winners were announced, so nobody had the chance to influence them.

Of course, Frankie and Carmen both knew the judges would be fully aware who provided their treats. Besides Bubble and Bake goodies, the judges would enjoy wood-fired pizzas from Paulo's Pizzeria on Dodge Street. Paulo and his brothers, Luca and Mario, had been baking authentic Neapolitan pizzas for ten years, constantly offering new varieties in different geometrical configurations. In Frankie's opinion, Paulo's was the best pizza in town, although a couple of popular chains had cropped up on Riverside Parkway, where the new developments were located.

Frankie checked the clock to see how time management was going for them. "Kelley LeVay will be here in an hour to pick up the bars, so at least that saves us a trip." The judges would convene at City Hall to determine the winners and munch on the goodies. "As usual, we'll finish just under the wire," Frankie sighed.

Carmen smirked. "Done is as good as done, Frankie. How many people are you expecting here tonight?"

"A lot," was Frankie's reply. "I haven't actually counted but I'm guessing around 30 or maybe more."

Jovie's eyes widened happily. "I'm so glad, Frankie. I was worried about the Christmas events with the mayor and council chairman gone, and you left to pull it all together. I know how stressed out you are about it, but with this many people helping, it should work out."

Frankie appreciated the support, admitting she had been in a constant tizzy since she was appointed chief organizer. "I just hope there's no arguing tonight. You know how some people can be when it comes to having their own way of doing things." Bonnie Fleisner's face appeared like an apparition. Of course, Peggy Champagne could be equally determined when she thought she was right.

Chapter Six

"Here, Frankie, drink this." Carmen pushed a custom purple Bubble and Bake mug into Frankie's hands. "And sit down, would you? All that pacing is making me jittery. You're worse than Elkie on patrol."

Frankie stopped, realizing for the first time that she'd been pacing the floor in the wine lounge for almost a half hour, altering her path every few minutes to peer out one of the shop windows. Now and then she caught a glimpse of the judges strolling down Meriwether and Granite streets, checking storefronts.

She laughed at Carmen's remark about the elkhound though. Elkie was an expert guard dog. Frankie caught Elkie parading past the large shop windows, first on the Meriwether side, then on the Granite. Every time the shop bell jingled, Elkie raised her head to judge whether the intruder was friend or foe.

With the expected hub of activity at the wine lounge, Frankie corralled Elkie outside on the deck with a fluffy blanket, water, and extra treats.

"Well, it's 6:45. They should be wrapping it up. I mean, how long can it take, anyway?" Frankie resumed her route to the shop window, pulled aside one large pine bough and peeked around its edge like a child playing hide and seek.

"Breathe, Frankie. Take a sip of your tea and sit down," Carmen tried again. "Since when are you so anxious about the decorating contest?" Carmen stood behind the lounge bar, wiping down glasses from the top shelf, so all was fresh for customers.

Frankie turned from the window, sat down on the window seat, and gave Carmen half of her attention. "Oh, it's not the contest. I'm watching for the business owners to get here for planning. Once the judges make their decision, they'll be coming here to announce the winners. I just want to be ready; that's all."

Frankie rose suddenly and abandoned her tea mug to greet Abe Arnold at the front door. Abe was editor of the *Whitman Watch*, the only newspaper in Whitman County. Tall and lean as a telephone pole, he was easy to locate in any crowd.

"Hello, Frankie," Abe said jovially, manhandling his large camera and a light stand. Abe preferred old-fashioned methods, using traditional camera equipment and a darkroom. He practiced the same kind of traditional reporting as well, carefully gathering information with a pencil and steno pad.

Although Abe employed two reporters, he always covered the choicest assignments, and any event tied to Deep Lakes Christmas was sure to receive his personal attention.

"Hi, Abe; are the judges close behind you, then?" Frankie wondered. She'd known the editor since he took over the paper a few years ago. Frankie wrote articles about grape cultivation, wine pairing, and special events held at Bubble and Bake. She'd hoped for a serious journalism job once upon a time, but that dream bubble had popped. So much for her Communications degree.

Abe was using his light meter and helped himself by flipping on the lounge lights for optimum photo conditions. "Should be here any time, I imagine." Then, changing the subject, Abe added, "Any updates for tomorrow's edition about Christmas events?"

Abe's routine question made Frankie's stomach churn; little beads of sweat began forming on the back of her neck. Being in charge wasn't as fun as Frankie originally thought, but she pasted on her composed face to reply.

"I'll have a lot more information for you after our planning meeting tonight. What's your deadline, Abe?" Frankie sounded self-assured on the outside despite the jiggling she inwardly felt.

"Look, if you can get me some details by 11, I'll save some space. It's going to be a late night anyway. Just call the office." Abe's attention shifted as the first wave of business owners walked into the shop, rubbing their cold hands, unwrapping their scarves, unzipping their jackets, and stamping their boots.

Good old Carmen had already placed the first round of pizzas on the bar top, and Jovie was right behind her with plates, napkins, and a tray of kringle wedges. Mood music played softly in the background, as Carmen and Jovie poured wine or popped open beers and sodas for the business owners.

Another wave of arriving business owners brought up the volume level considerably, but everyone fell as silent as a church congregation when the three judges came through the shop door, easily recognizable by their judges' badges.

Fire Captain Phil Mortensen started conversing easily with Abe as he handed the editor what was likely a list of soon-to-be announced winners. Phil was a fixture at local events, a dependable volunteer for grilling brats at summer festivals, manning the firemen's dunk tank on July 4th, or now, judging decorations and anything else required for the Christmas festivities.

Judge number two, former mayor Stanley Gray, stood off to the side and alternated between staring out the window or at his feet. Gray served three terms as mayor, and it was hard to imagine anyone more awkward in the limelight than he had been. A former museum archivist from Springfield, Illinois, Stanley's white complexion testified he spent little time in the light, just as his quiet demeanor suggested he spent more time with artifacts than living, breathing objects. Frankie recalled how relieved he'd been when Adele Lundgren decided to run for mayor. Needless to say, Adele ran unopposed.

The third judge paraded to the staging area by the fireplace mantle where Abe had set up a microphone and small awards table. As round as she was tall, school administrator Gloria Senger strode forward as if she owned the place and pulled three trophies from the satchel she carried, standing them on the table. Looking business-smart yet festive in her berry-red skirt and jacket, she rolled her shoulders back like a prizefighter preparing for action and tapped the microphone for attention.

All eyes focused on Gloria, who was clearly comfortable being in charge. Gloria offered her cheshire cat smile framed in berry-red lipstick that matched her suit and invited Phil and Stanley to join her at the table.

Gloria's voice sounded like a fanfare. "On behalf of our mayor, Adele Lundgren, I'd like to welcome you to the kickoff of our beloved Deep Lakes Christmas tradition of December festivities." Gloria and Adele were cut from the same cloth, both hardworking, no-nonsense women; the two had become fast friends when Gloria moved to town a couple of years ago.

"Judges Mortensen, Gray, and I were impressed by the decorations we saw tonight representing the Victorian theme. You should all be proud of your efforts in sprucing up our little town and making it an inviting place for visitors to spend some time and money this season."

Gloria didn't mince words. Frankie suspected that Gloria, who hailed from Milwaukee, saw Deep Lakes as a bumpkin-filled burg that would only be too grateful for some foot traffic during the holidays. And, she was at least half-right. Deep Lakes thrived on summer tourism, made do in the autumn because of fall colors and deer hunting, revived in the spring as the fishing season and warmer weather began, but barely survived the quiet season of winter. Most businesses hoped for any last gasp of life the holidays offered.

"We can't wait to see what you have to offer shoppers starting tomorrow with our extended 'after dark' hours. I know the Healys have many visitors signed up for their wreath and gnome making workshop tomorrow night at Shamrock Floral, but there's many more new offerings this year, too." Gloria was settling in and had obviously veered off script, and Frankie was surprised when Stanley Gray cleared his throat meaningfully and gently touched Gloria's elbow.

Unflappable, Gloria didn't miss a beat. "Of course, all of you will want to take a stack of flyers listing all our events and participating vendors," she cooed. "I've placed them at the end of the bar." Gloria pointed where Carmen was standing and as if on cue, Carmen smiled brightly and held up a flyer from the pile. " Without further ado, we'd like to present the awards for this year's best decorated businesses."

As announcements proceeded, Stanley Gray handed off the third-place trophy, an inscribed bronze reindeer, to Frankie's neighbor, Rachel Engebretsen. Rachel rented the Meriwether Street side of Frankie's building, and operated the Bead Me, I'm Yours craft shop.

Rachel and many local crafters banded together to create a handmade display of spruce branches trimmed with orange slices hanging from twine and old sheet music folded into bows, three-dimensional bells, fans, stars and paper chains. Ropes of clove studded pears and oranges along with carved limes, pomegranates, and cinnamon sticks hung from the top of the window frame. Lace covered cone-shaped baskets held crafting supplies like spools of ribbon, skeins of embroidery floss, and tubes of colored beads. All in all, it was the perfect invitation for shoppers to come in and buy supplies to make their own Victorian decorations.

Rachel smiled happily for the camera as Frankie gave her an approving wave. The young brunette, who preferred flannel and jeans and wore her long hair pulled back with a headband, was dressed up for the occasion in a tribal print maxi skirt and loosely knit dark red sweater, her hair hanging in loose curls. She'd been Frankie's renter for a couple of years and was making a small living, thanks to the workshops, paint nights and weekly knitting club she hosted.

Captain Phil stepped forward, an emblem of strength and classical fireman's calendar good looks. He held the silver reindeer award like a fire hose, aimed horizontally at the audience. Frankie tried not to smile too much, but imagined that all eyes were on Phil's handsome face and physique, so it was unlikely anyone noticed where the trophy was pointed.

Phil clapped Mike Hansen on the shoulder as he handed the 2nd place award to Lori Hansen for the couple's classic Victorian inn, Hotel Divine, on Doty Street. The Hansens restored the 1800's hotel a few years back, choosing to keep the original owners' name for it. True to tradition, every window in the hotel glowed with a single lit candle taper. The front bay window featured a tall fir tree with lit tin-pressed candles—flameless of course—on its branches, trimmed in red velvet bows. The window display was filled with porcelain tea pots in various Christmas designs poised on an antique tatted tablecloth. Interspersed among the teapots, in various poses, were vintage elves with impish smiles.

Business owners looked on in appreciation and applauded the choice. Mike and Lori were resident antique experts, and almost every Deep Lakes citizen relied on them at some point to answer their questions about a family heirloom or garage sale find.

Gloria wasted no time in assuming her front-and-center post as soon as Abe finished snapping photos of the couple and fire captain. She practically stepped on Phil's shoes in the process of snatching the golden reindeer award before eagerly grabbing the microphone in one hand. "And now, the moment we've been waiting for," Gloria began. Frankie and Carmen couldn't resist exchanging eye rolls. What did Gloria think this was—the Oscars?

"The first place Golden Reindeer trophy for the best decorated business of the holiday season, and the coveted position of Grand Marshal for the holiday parade goes to—Glen and Meredith Healy of Shamrock Floral!"

A big fan of the florists, Frankie clapped loudly. The first place honor wasn't a huge surprise to anyone, since the Healys were specialists in decorating and offered their consulting services to townspeople about house and yard decor.

Frankie and her crew admired Shamrock Floral's picture window when they walked back from the Mud Puppy earlier that week. They marveled at the life-sized Father Christmas carrying a small decorated tree, a large velvet sack of toys at his feet. Parked beside him was a silver and white sleigh with two reindeer ready for takeoff. Red jingle bells hung around their harnesses and silver balls dangled from their antlers. The sleigh was filled with Poinsettias in every color: red, pink, white; some were even dyed blue and violet.

Photos completed, Abe packed up his equipment, and the business owners divided themselves into committees, first grabbing fresh pieces of pizza and kringle and beverages of choice. They headed in different directions to claim a space in the wine lounge. Frankie's smile could not be contained. What a perfect idea.

She managed to catch up to Captain Phil as he was about to leave. "Hey, Phil. Good job judging this year." Frankie had to look way up to meet the eyes of the tall fireman.

"Well, thanks, Frankie. I think it went well. You never

know if you're going to hurt someone's feelings, but hey, we all agreed on the winners."

"Quick question," Frankie began. "I'm planning to call Bob from Snowy Ridge tomorrow. I just want to make sure the fire department has equipment ready at Spurgeon Park for the town tree?"

"Yep. Everything's ready to go. We hauled most of it over there this afternoon. The guys will be stringing lights and hoisting the star at our next weekly meeting. It's going to be a marathon session," Phil grinned, obviously absorbed in the holiday spirit.

Frankie commended the fire captain's dedication. Both Phil and his Kindergarten teacher spouse, Jenny, stepped up frequently to lead projects and help with festival events. Frankie knew Jenny would be helping the youngest gingerbread house designers with filling icing tubes and sorting decorative candies.

Frankie impulsively grabbed a bottle of Winter Dreams from the shelf. "Here, take this home to share with Jenny and—Merry Christmas." The couple often visited the wine lounge during the summer, bringing out-of-town friends and family to patronize the shop. Phil regularly placed bakery orders for department meetings.

"Wow, that's very nice of you, Frankie. I'm sure we'll enjoy this." Phil held the bottle aloft and headed out the door, just as signs of discord were on the rise.

Bonnie Fleisner and the rest of the ice rink/ice carving committee were arguing in twos and threes, clearly divided about how to proceed with the numerous tasks before them. Frankie came over with her reliable yellow notepad and pen just in time to see Bonnie wagging a finger under Kerby Hahn's nose.

"If you and Steffie are going to be on my committee, you're going to have to listen to the way we do things. I've been working on the ice rink and carving event for years, after all."

Oh great—leave it to Bonnie to draw first blood at the planning meeting, Frankie thought. Out loud she said, "How can I help out? Let's hear what you've all decided so far." Frankie offered an encouraging smile and patted Steffie's arm.

Bonnie glared at Kerby, tattling accusingly, "*He* thinks we should have a hot cocoa bar and a kettle corn vendor at the ice rink. We've never done that before."

Frankie thought the idea was fresh and would go over well with visitors. Kerby said he had a friend in Green Lake who made kettle corn at fairs and festivals statewide. He was sure his friend would be happy to bring his kettle corn stand to Deep Lakes.

"So, what do the rest of you think about it?" Having dealt with a variety of customer complaints, Frankie was practiced in diplomacy.

The other committee members deemed both ideas agreeable. Lori Hansen was excited about the possibilities of a hot cocoa bar. "We can offer all kinds of varieties like peppermint, white chocolate, caramel, and different toppings, too," Lori enthused, looking around at the nodding heads. It appeared Bonnie Fleisner was like the proverbial cheese from "The Farmer in the Dell"—standing alone.

Mike Hansen added the idea of offering hot pretzels with cheese sauce or pizza sauce; "you know, like they offer at the mall." More heads nodded as Mike asked Kerby: "Do you know anyone who can make pretzels or does your kettle corn guy know anyone, since he travels the circuit?" Kerby said he'd make a call to his friend.

Bonnie was determined to get back to her list of items that needed to be done to ready the ice rink area for the ice sculpture festival. She began rapid firing the list in her take-charge voice. The committee members divided the tasks while Bonnie noted the assignments. Just when Frankie was satisfied that the committee was back on track, another argument ensued over who would take charge of keeping the rink cleared.

Frankie told the committee that after Christmas, local organizations took turns hosting weekend skating at the rink for the winter season, if she remembered correctly. Each organization readied the rink, rented skates, and furnished concessions as a moneymaker for their group. She wondered if those groups could be contacted to volunteer to clear the rink on a schedule. After all, the ice sculpting festival was a week away; how much snow could possibly fall in that short of time?

Bonnie glared at Frankie, clearly peeved by her interference.

"We simply can't ask organizations to get involved with this. No, no, no . . . that won't do at all," Bonnie sounded waspish.

"Maybe some high schoolers who need community service would be willing to do it," Mike Hansen proposed.

Bonnie bristled, nostrils flaring like a bull. "Hymph, good luck with that."

"I'll call the school and ask. I work with a number of high schoolers." Mike was part of the athletic foundation for the Flames, Deep Lakes' school mascot. "Let me see what I can do."

His offer was met with an even deeper glare from Bonnie and a second disapproving grunt, but she said no more.

Frankie took advantage of the stalemate to continue making the rounds to other areas. She noticed the parade committee was a conglomeration of transportation-related businesses and wondered if that was Adele's idea. The committee's lineup included: P and S Farm Implement, Triple Crown Marine, Rob's Holiday Stationstore, Deep Lakes Auto Center, Julson's Towing Service, Lake Life RV Sales and Service, and Rowley's Boats and Bicycles. Frankie counted 13 members, sitting closely with their heads together, chatting amiably, most of them tossing back beers. Clearly, this group had worked together before.

At best, Frankie was merely acquainted with many of them; some she didn't even know by name, but she only cared that they were accomplishing the task of organizing the parade. Frankie wondered if her best move was to keep her distance and let them be, but she worried she might be perceived as disrespectful, a trait Peggy Champagne's daughter couldn't bear.

Smiling brightly, Frankie bounced over to the group. "Some of you might not know me, so I wanted to introduce myself. I'm Frankie Champagne, and I can't tell you how happy I am that you all came by tonight."

Collective nods and smiles moved like a wave among the group. One dashing, well-groomed man in dress jeans and a button-down shirt extended his hand toward Frankie's. "Jake Robbins. I'm the general manager at Triple Crown. Thanks for hosting us tonight." Jake looked to be in the latter half of his 30's, and was polished in the PR department. "Well done on the snacks, by the way. Your kringle is to die for, Frankie."

It appeared Jake Robbins was the spokesman for the committee, designated or otherwise. Since nobody else looked ready to speak, Frankie offered to refresh drinks and asked how the parade was coming together.

Jake didn't have much to say on the subject, passing the torch to Rob Nelson, an old-timer in parade planning. Rob had been running the Holiday Stationstore since the 1970's and might have been an original parade planner for the event's tenure.

Rob looked up from his beer when his wife, Sandy, elbowed him. Looking directly at him and speaking loudly, Sandy pointed a thumb at Frankie. "She wants to know how the parade plans are coming along."

Rob was aging and had developed a little shakiness in his voice and mannerisms. He raised keen blue eyes at Frankie, confident in his ability to lead parade planning. "Going just fine," he said in a folksy way. "Same as ever." Rob's shoulders hunched up to his large ears as if to indicate more details were unnecessary; everything was in order. Frankie would just have to trust in the committee, for she hadn't seen the holiday parade since her daughters were little. She tried another tack.

"Abe from the newspaper asked me for the lowdown on holiday events, so could you elaborate a little?" Frankie's eyes darted around the group members; anyone who could provide details would do.

Sandy pulled a piece of paper out of a folder and handed it to Frankie. "Maybe this will help. It's the parade lineup. You can have it; it's an extra copy."

Now why couldn't Sandy have just done that in the first place? Frankie wondered why it was like pulling teeth to get the locals to be more forthcoming. Before she could take the proffered list, however, Jake Robbins intercepted it.

"Wait a minute, Rob and Sandy. Have the groups on this list all been contacted? I mean, this paper says 2017 on top..." Jake looked confused, and his confusion made Frankie rethink her first impression that the committee members were on the same page.

Rob raised his head slowly and stared at Jake as if he were an intruder. "Don't need to. They'll be here, just like every year." His low measured voice didn't invite contradiction. Frankie assumed Jake was a newcomer to the committee, and this year just might be his last year of service.

Jake handed the parade list to Frankie and silently crept back to his chair. Chatter resumed among the veterans in the group, mostly talk of fishing, hunting, RV's, and cars. Frankie admonished herself for thinking the committee powwow was about parade plans. This seemed more like a bull session.

She walked back to the bar area where Carmen was busily pouring wine and handing out beers to the business owners. Raising her eyebrows sharply at Frankie, she said, "You know how much free wine and beer we're giving away? I mean, I like the holidays and all, but do I look like Santa Claus?" Carmen wasn't one to mince words.

Frankie perused the open wine bottles behind the bar and looked in the beer cooler. There were six open wine varieties and the beer cooler was half-empty. Frankie wished the committees were as enthused about planning holiday events as they were about eating free food and drinking free alcohol. "I think it's about time to pull the plug on this free-for-all," she grimaced. "Did we serve all the food we'd planned on serving?"

Carmen nodded. "And then some. Jovie made a few extra pizzas. The last of them are on the bartop."

"Okay. I've checked in with two of the three committees here. I'll just check in with the third, but first, I'm going to announce the last call for free alcohol—in as nice a way as possible."

Frankie turned toward the group, stood on a nearby coffee table to be more visible, made a circle with her thumb and forefinger, and whistled loudly, just the way her brothers had taught her. The din of voices stopped immediately; all eyes were on Frankie.

"Hey everyone. I just wanted to thank you for coming tonight and for your hard work." Inwardly, she cringed at her own sugar-coated compliment. "It looks like you're accomplishing your planning for the holiday events, and I think we're going to have a great season." She smiled enthusiastically around the room, activating her inner cheerleader.

"There's still a few pieces of pizza on the bar and a little wine left before we call it a night. My staff and I are going to start cleaning up now, and we sure hope to see you all again soon." Frankie hoped that sounded tactful. She glanced at her mother, the Miss Manners expert, gauging her reaction. Peggy nodded at Frankie meaningfully and sported a smile of satisfaction.

Frankie walked over to her mother's committee, the tree lighting ceremony and Holly-Days group. This was the largest committee since so much went into the three-day festival. The historical society was in charge of the musical entertainment and sleigh rides through the park, but Peggy appeared to be the only society member present.

Jan and Sheila Zinski, co-owners of Sterling Creek Supper Club, were involved in active conversation with a couple of other restaurant owners and the Karlsens, who ran the Wisconsin Specialties shop across the street from Bubble and Bake. The cluster appeared to have the food and drink portion of Holly-Days well in hand.

The rest of the committee divided up the tasks of sorting through the family activities, contests, and prizes. Frankie and Carmen were not part of the committee, but the shop sponsored and hosted the gingerbread contest on Saturday of the festival.

Frankie scooted a chair between Beau Collins, manager of Deep 6 Cinema and Jill Johnson, owner of Treasury of Books. Jill was taking notes for the group, and Frankie wanted to make certain she had a list of decorating items local businesses could drop off for the gingerbread contest.

Jill's business management skills were impeccable, yet her creativity was evident in the book store's displays and author events. Frankie dropped by whenever she could to find a gift for someone or a book for herself from her growing "must-read" list. She loved Treasury's nooks, inviting visitors to camp out and read. The children's section changed with the seasons and the holidays. Currently a curtain of snowflakes dangled from the ceiling; white sparkly cloth lay in folds around artificial pines, where stuffed woodland animals posed or perched, and real wooden tree stumps served as stools for little ones.

Jill looked up at Frankie and began reciting from her notes. Bright red glittery reading glasses perching on her pointy nose, Jill began, "So, I have down here that the shop is looking for any edible items that can be used for decorating gingerbread: candies, pretzels, sandwich cookies, crackers, marshmallows, etc. Anything else you need?" Jill's wide brown eyes peered above the readers, expectantly.

"I don't think so. The shop always provides the gingerbread, icing, decorating bags and tools, plus hot cider and hot cocoa for the participants," Frankie said proudly. She and Carmen had originated the contest and hosted it the past five years. It was their baby.

Frankie easily garnered information for the newspaper from Jill, ignored Beau Collins as he sidled up closer than necessary to Frankie, then moved to another table to check in with her mother, who was repeatedly fidgeting with her napkin. Peggy Champagne did not fidget.

"Mother?" Frankie began and didn't have to say more.

"I just don't know where we're going to find a sleigh. I've checked around the county. Of course, the Linde farm will provide their draft horses as they've always done, but they only have the hay wagon we've used in the past—no sleigh." Peggy looked at Frankie, then at the other committee members, as if one of them should have an answer for her.

Frankie suspected this line of conversation had been raised and exhausted before she ever showed up at their table, but Peggy was not one to give up easily. Frankie certainly didn't know where to find a sleigh, a relic from another era, so she changed the subject.

"What about the music? Do you have a lineup for the weekend?" Frankie was sure she'd entered safe territory, especially when all the members perked up.

Peggy handed her daughter the entertainment list for the weekend, featuring an array of musicians to please every age and taste. Frankie was happy to see an ensemble from The Capital Youth Orchestra would perform after the tree lighting and lead the town in carol singing. Sharmaine's helpful suggestion had paid off.

But Sarah Callahan, the receptionist at Callahan Realty, looked flustered. Frankie gestured in her direction, an invitation for her to speak her mind.

"I think some of the entertainment you lined up is outdated. I mean, it's time for some new blood, if you know what I mean." Sarah was young and ambitious, like the rest of the Callahan family. Her blonde head swiveled toward Peggy Champagne and the other older women beside her, as if in accusation. Frankie held her breath, knowing that those three women were a force to be reckoned with.

The blocky frame of Marjean Van Dyke, insurance agency manager, rose from the chair she occupied to stand a full five-foot-three inches over the lovely Sarah.

"Now just a minute, young lady." Marjean wore the face of a prison warden. "Everybody in town loves these bands, and that's why we're going to continue to have them."

Margo Ness, business partner with her brother, Stuart, at Ness Travels, tagged in while Marjean continued her intimidating stance over Sarah. "Marjean is right, Sarah. I've been organizing the music with these ladies for years, and we receive high praise for the entertainment…" she paused, then raised her voice sharply, "very high praise. Besides, you can't just come in at the last minute and try to change things."

Sarah began to stand up and lifted one high-heeled foot meaningfully in the direction of Marjean's orthopedic shoes. Before Sarah could pounce, however, Peggy placed a firm hand on her arm.

"Sarah, you may have a point about the entertainment. And, we'd love to hear your ideas for next year. It's always good to have a fresh perspective. But, I'm afraid Margo and Marjean are right. There's not enough time to make changes to the lineup. We're only one week away."

Sarah reluctantly sat down, then pushed her empty wine glass toward Frankie with an exaggerated pout. "Do you have any more of this? I could use another glass." Frankie politely took the glass back to the bar where she sniffed it, recognized the flavor, and poured from a bottle of a red variety that closely matched it from the open bottles.

Less than an hour later, Frankie and Carmen turned

off the shop lights except for the Christmas displays, and emptied one leftover Hygge Holiday into two glasses.

"That didn't go quite as I imagined, Carmen. I'm not sure we're going to be able to pull off the holiday events this year," Frankie sighed.

"And by 'we' you mean the town, correct? Because this isn't on you, Frankie," Carmen reminded her friend. "It's going to be what it's going to be, and you're going to have to let it go, my friend."

Even though Frankie knew Carmen was right, it didn't change the fact she desperately wanted the holiday events to run smoothly and be successful. Why couldn't she be like Adele, who ran the city and all its happenings with finesse and adroitness? Suddenly the Christmas spark had fizzled, and Frankie felt swallowed by the darkness.

After she bade Jovie and Carmen good night, Frankie jotted down Jovie's time schedule for the rest of the weekend on the kitchen's whiteboard. At least she would have the extra help to fill orders and bake ahead.

Frankie stuck a post-it on the counter reminding herself to call her mother to see if she could take more shifts in the wine lounge. The note called to mind Carmen's suggestion that Peggy had repaired the broken angel.

Frankie padded quietly to the Christmas tree, having grabbed the step ladder from the hall closet. She flipped one light switch, illuminating half the lounge, climbed up, and carefully took down the angel. This angel, although identical to Frankie's broken one, was completely intact, without any visible glue ridges or hairline cracks.

"Well, what do you know about this, Elkie?" Frankie asked, looking down at the canine, who had followed her.

Frankie put the step ladder away, looked in the lounge and hallway waste baskets for the broken angel, but found no evidence. Hands on her hips, Frankie stared down the dog accusingly. "Well?" she asked. But Elkie's poker face gave away nothing.

Frankie brought her laptop to one of the high top tables where she could look out the window at the town holiday lights, hoping for a resurgence of spirit. She pulled her notes together, such as they were, from the various committees and began an article for Abe Arnold. Elkie was lying under the table at her feet, softly snoring, until the shop bell jingled quietly, causing the hound to woof in warning.

It was Alonzo, still in his sheriff uniform. Elkie rose, trotted over to sniff Alonzo, and licked his hand in greeting. Frankie was dumbfounded by Elkie's friendliness.

"Hi, Frankie. I thought I'd stop by, since I saw you in the window." Alonzo looked a little confused as he eased his broad frame onto the high chair. "I came to see how the holiday meeting went . . . and what are you doing with Garrett Iverson's dog?"

Chapter Seven

"Garrett Iverson? The coroner?" Frankie's jaw hit the floor.

Alonzo nodded, an amused smile on his face. "Yes, that Garrett Iverson, unless you know another one?" He lifted one finger midair, remembering, "Matter of fact, he mentioned the other day that his dog was missing." Alonzo drew both brows together.

Frankie stared ahead, momentarily lost in thought. "Well I, I don't know. This dog showed up in the backyard by the creek, cold, hungry, and worn out. I took her to Dr. Sadie. She wasn't chipped and didn't have an ID—the dog, I mean."

Alonzo offered to take the elkhound off Frankie's hands and deliver her to Garrett, but Frankie raised her hands in protest.

"No, not necessary, Lon. I put myself in charge of this foundling. I'll call Garrett Iverson and make arrangements to bring her back home in the morning." She raised her chin defiantly, that old independence asserting itself.

Alonzo sat up straighter in his seat. "Oh, that's right. You've met Garrett, haven't you?" Alonzo wondered if Frankie's desire to return the dog revealed an interest in the man, and he wasn't sure he liked that idea. "He helped you out of a jam at the winery the other day."

Frankie's dander rose a notch. "Well, I wouldn't call it a jam exactly . . . and he helped me and Carmen . . . well, you called him, Alonzo!" She couldn't figure out why Alonzo was making her feel defensive.

Alonzo raised his hands in surrender. "Methinks the lady doth protest too much," he said quietly. Thankfully, Frankie sank back into her seat, relaxed, and blew out a sigh. Alonzo was like a brother to her, and she recovered quickly from their verbal spats.

The two played catch-up over a couple of brews, as Alonzo helped himself to the remaining pieces of cold pizza still sitting on the bar. Frankie switched topics to the town's mysterious visitors.

"Hey, Lon. I've been meaning to ask you, what do you know about the train coming through town a few nights ago? Weird, huh?"

Alonzo looked at her like she had a screw loose. "What are you talking about, Frankie? I don't know anything about that," Alonzo was certain.

Frankie described Jewel and shared her story of the train having to stop in Deep Lakes because it could go no farther due to the snowstorm. She found it hard to believe that the Whitman County Sheriff's Department wasn't part of the railway's notification policy.

Lon slugged the rest of his Spotted Cow beer. "I think the holiday stress is getting to you, Frankie," he said, eyes twinkling. "A gnome lady? A train in Deep Lakes?" Lon chuckled.

"Carmen called her a gnome lady, not me. I was just trying to describe her. You mean you haven't heard anything from anyone else in town about Jewel or the train?" Frankie imagined other residents must have seen Jewel around town. She had to be eating somewhere, shopping perhaps. Of course, Frankie recalled that she herself still hadn't met Forrest, Jewel's husband.

Alonzo shook his head and glanced toward the cooler, wondering if he should have a second brew.

Frankie blew out a long breath. "Well, look at the shop decorations. Most of those were made by Jewel. You can ask Carmen. Chloe, Sharmaine, and Jovie met her, too . . . I'm not losing it, Lon." Frankie raised that defiant chin again.

She and Lon had been friends since high school and grew even closer after Frankie's divorce many years ago. Frankie related to Lon the way she related to her four brothers; she needed to assert her independence but counted on his care and reliability just the same. Lon may have other notions about his relationship with Frankie, however. The good sheriff found himself thinking on and off if he and Frankie could be an item. But Lon was well aware that Frankie was not a woman to be pushed, so he never seemed to find the right way to broach the subject.

He rose off the chair now and donned his heavy jacket. It was getting late, and Frankie still had an article to file with the newspaper. Besides, it was snowing again. Lon's radio buzzed on his belt. Dispatch was offering a weather report, and it wasn't promising.

"Looks like we're in for another blast from Old Man Winter. Could be a long night—hope we won't need lights and sirens." After saying good night, Alonzo couldn't resist adding, "I hope this storm doesn't bring another train through town."

She gave Alonzo a quick hug, punching his arm as she did so.

* * *

Frankie was up by 4 a.m., speculating about Garrett's reaction to her having his dog. She showered and dressed quickly, then peered out the window with her face pressed to the glass into the darkness. She flipped the deck light on and grimaced. There was a lot of fresh snow on the ground to tend to, and small light flakes were still falling. She snapped off the light again and headed downstairs to feed Elkie, leaving the orphaned feline slumbering peacefully by the stove.

Elkie pawed at the kitchen door where Frankie had set the espresso machine into motion. By the looks of the weather, she needed a heavy dose of java to power her through the shoveling alone. Elkie pushed through the swinging doors before Frankie had the chance to let her in, leash grasped between her teeth. She wagged her tail at Frankie, bent her head down, and greeted her with a friendly woof.

Keeping her canine promise, Frankie walked Elkie in the cold crisp air, using the road as their footpath. There was nothing much visible but the swirling puffs of their exhales, one a few feet off the ground, the other, just a bit higher. They measured their exhales in unison, both feeling much better for the morning exercise.

Amid the quietly falling flakes of snow, they circled back to Bubble and Bake. With a thick double coat of fur, the elkhound was made for snow and clearly in her element, rolling around and sticking her face here and there in the fresh snow as the mood struck her.

Frankie laughed despite the shoveling ahead of her. She guessed nearly a foot of white stuff was piled on top of the already substantial blanket. In the misty light of a half moon, she brushed snow off the bird feeders to make them ready for breakfast at daybreak. The snow had slowed to a spitting shower with tiny ice particles hitting the windows and Frankie's face.

In spite of herself, Frankie felt tears forming in the corners of her eyes. She didn't realize how much Elkie had touched her heart in one day. She bent down to nuzzle the hound's ears and neck. "Okay, back to business, Elkie. I need to get busy here and then get you back home."

Frankie decided to call Garrett around six o'clock, hoping that was a reasonable hour.

She suspected the trip to Deep Lakes would be slow-going again for Chloe and Sharmaine, and she decided to send them texts to take their time getting there. She hoped the two would travel in Sharmaine's Tucson instead of Chloe's compact car, which had been in and out of the mechanic's a lot lately. The day was shaping up to be another quiet one at the shop as the town moved in slow motion.

* * *

Frankie felt a tingling warmth coursing through her body as she tapped in Garrett Inverson's phone number. What was going on with her, she wondered, as she inhaled deeply to slow her quaking pulse. A friendly deep voice picked up.

"Hello, this is Garrett."

Frankie's voice came out in a stammer. "Oh yes, hello. This is Frankie. Frankie Champagne." She paused, but hearing no recognition, she went on, more businesslike.

"You may not remember, but we met the other day when you rescued me out at my vineyard . . . well, not rescued really, but you helped me and my partner Carmen when our van wouldn't start . . . and . . ."

The Golden Firefly had emerged from parts unknown to give Frankie a little snap in her ear. "Get a grip, Francine. You're just trying to return his dog. This isn't a job interview or the dating game . . ."

Garrett cut off Goldie before she could finish her

admonishment. "Of course I remember you, Frankie," Garrett spoke as if Frankie was a celebrity of some sort, and she wasn't sure how to read his words.

"Well, thank you again for helping us out." Her voice and heart rate were back in check. "The reason I'm calling you is: I think I have your dog. She's a Norweigian elkhound who showed up here yesterday by the creek behind the shop. Alonzo is pretty sure she's your hound."

"Yes, I've been looking for Freya for a couple of days. She ran off chasing something down the river after the last storm, and I haven't seen her since," he said, excitedly. Frankie was happy to hear the warmth in his voice toward his missing dog.

"Well, I just took her out for a romp—on a leash of course. Anyway, if you give me your address, I'll deliver her home." Inwardly, Frankie followed a fiery impulse to see where Garrett lived.

Garrett gave his fire number on County WH east of town but wondered if Frankie should be out on the roads. "You know, the plow has only made a couple of passes. I just finished plowing out my driveway so I can make it into work. Maybe I should come by and pick up Freya."

An outside force seemed to be driving Frankie's actions today. "Oh no, that isn't necessary. I have an SUV, and I'm used to driving in the snow. Besides, you'll have to just turn around and take Freya back home. Let me save you the trip."

"All right then. I'll be watching for you." He spoke with hesitation followed by surrender. Garrett Iverson didn't know the force of Frankie Champagne's determination.

She readied Freya and started the SUV as Carmen drove down the alley. Frankie was thrilled to see the twins in the van and hoped they had come along to do some shoveling. She waved enthusiastically.

"Good morning, Carmen, Kyle, Carlos."

"School is delayed again. I figured the boys would be useful down here with the snow shovels," Carmen began. "You know, we really need to buy a snow blower. Maybe we should look at Fleisner's." Seeing the running SUV, she asked, "Are you going somewhere?"

Frankie nodded. "I'm taking Elkie home. Well actually, her name is Freya."

"Wait a minute. Last night you didn't know where the dog came from, and now you know, this early in the morning?" Carmen wondered.

Frankie faltered just a tad. "We-ell, last night Alonzo stopped by after closing, and he recognized the dog. She belongs to Garrett Iverson." Frankie gazed off in the distance at nothing in particular, and Carmen noticed.

"So, you're taking a field trip out to his house, eh?" Carmen moved toward her business partner in an attempt to look her in the eyes.

Frankie raised her own eyes then. "It makes sense, Carmen. He can't bring the dog to work with him, after all."

"Why is your face so red, Frankie?" Carmen jabbed her friend, but quickly added, "I want a full report when you get back."

After Frankie loaded up Freya, she rolled down the window and called after Carmen's retreating back. "Hey, Carmie! I told Chloe and Sharmaine to take their time getting here. I figure it will be a slow day. I haven't fed Cookie Cat yet, and Jewel is supposed to stop by for a kringle. It's on the back counter." Carmen gave an exaggerated nod of her hooded parka, and Frankie drove off.

Although Garrett lived a few miles out of town, navigating the snow-covered roads slowed Frankie down. She had to pay attention to fire numbers to find his driveway, so it was a good 15 minutes or more when she pulled into a long gravel driveway in the middle of two empty fields that rose upward to an old Victorian-style farmstead of cream brick. Wide, painted wooden steps ascended to the large front porch featuring decorative columns with spider-web-designed corner pieces. The indoor-outdoor carpeting was worn and the decorative trim above the gothic windows needed work, but the house was a classic, formerly owned by Sheriff Nelson, who had served Whitman County for 20 years. The wrought iron trimmed door opened before Frankie could press the bell.

Freya barked in delight at the sight of her master. Frankie felt almost like an intruder at their joyful reunion, seeing Garrett's warm brown eyes alight with delight for his hound.

"There, there, Girl." Garrett lovingly hugged Freya's neck. "Thanks so much for returning her. Come on in, and I'll give you the tour," Garrett invited. "I'm working on the interior in pieces and plan to start on the outside next summer," he informed her.

Frankie admired the hardwood floors, ornate bannister on the central staircase, and wainscoting trim. Garrett was currently removing old wallpaper, painting walls, and restoring the ivory and gold patterned tin ceiling on the first story. The kitchen was completely remodeled with antique-looking distressed oak cabinets and dark red granite countertops. Frankie gasped at the finished room.

"I'll take that as a compliment, Frankie. I like to putter around with carpentry. I learned a lot from my dad and uncles," Garrett shared.

"You did all of this yourself?" When he nodded, Frankie beamed. "This is just beautiful, Garrett. Well done." To further explain her worthy praise, she added, "My father owned a construction company, so I've seen a lot of new and remodeled places in my life."

Garrett checked the time, suggested he should probably think of leaving for work, then escorted Frankie to the porch, Freya in tow. "Guess I better let Freya out one more time before I head into town."

Frankie wanted to ask him about the dog's name, and

now was as good a time as any. "So, Freya. Is she named for the Norse goddess?"

"She is, indeed. Goddess of love and beauty. At least, I think she's a beauty." Garrett playfully cuffed the dog's ears.

"She is a beauty for sure. But Freya was also a goddess of sorcery," Frankie tossed out the offhand comment casually.

Garrett smiled brightly. "How do you know so much about Norse mythology?"

Frankie explained that her grandmother, Sophie Petersen, enjoyed sharing some of the stories she grew up with as a little girl in Denmark. "Grandma Sophie taught me the art of baking. I have many of her recipes, and sometimes I can hear her voice while I'm rolling out dough."

Frankie was lost for the moment, fondly recalling time spent with her grandma, the woman who sewed and embroidered her very first apron. Frankie still used Grandma Sophie's wooden rolling pin, and kept it oiled so it would outlive her. Frankie imagined the day when her grandmother's rolling pin would be passed on to her own children or grandchildren.

Garrett looked softly upon this red-haired woman, wondering about her life, wanting to know more about her. "From what I hear about your bakery, your grandma must have taught you well."

Frankie blushed, not from Garrett's praise, but because she had forgotten to bring bakery to Garrett, as was her custom almost every time she ventured to someone's home.

"I left so quickly this morning, I forgot to bring you something from the shop. I'm sorry."

Garrett waved away her apology. By now, the two had wandered behind the house where Freya had trotted. Both noticed the hound was nowhere to be seen, and Garrett began whistling and calling while Frankie looked around.

Straight ahead was an old barn where Frankie headed while Garrett veered left toward the garage. Noises were coming from the barn, so Frankie pushed open the door and let herself in. Besides a tractor with a snow-covered plow blade hooked up to it, there was a skid loader, and something behind it that caught Frankie's eye. Scooting between the machinery, she gasped as an old horse-drawn sleigh came into view. There was Freya, sitting on the seat, tongue hanging out with what appeared to be a big smile on her face.

"You are the goddess of sorcery, aren't you, Freya?" The hound presented her customary head nod that Frankie had come to recognize. "Well, let's have a look at this sleigh and see what kind of shape it's in." Remembering Garrett was still outside looking around, she called out loudly: "Garrett, Freya's in here. Can you come here, please?"

Garrett laughed when he saw Frankie and Freya sitting on the sleigh seat. "Well, what have we here?"

"Okay, weird question. My mother is actually trying

to find a sleigh. Any chance this one's in any shape to be part of the Holly-Days event? The town wants to offer sleigh rides through Spurgeon Park."

Garrett stroked his short goatee methodically. "I'm not sure. The sleigh came with the property." Frankie looked ever so hopefully at Garrett, and so did Freya. He walked around the sleigh, assessing what he could. "The runners look good. They'll need to be cleaned of the rust, but that's not a hard job. I need to find an old farmer to look at the frame and axles to be sure they're in good shape, though." Frankie was still silent, wearing an expectant expression.

"Okay, Miss Francine. I'll make it a priority to find someone to get this contraption running by . . . When do you need it?"

"Next weekend. Thank you, Garrett. This is amazing!" Frankie gave the elkhound a warm hug around the neck. "And thank you especially, Freya, for leading me out here."

"Now don't get too far ahead yet, Frankie. I can't promise the sleigh will be in operation, but I will do my best." Garrett's irresistible smile and roasted chestnut eyes said otherwise. Somehow, he would find a way to deliver the sleigh for the Holly-Days.

Chapter Eight

Frankie was normally a cautious driver, but she couldn't contain her excitement about the sleigh, so she gave into her urge and pressed in her mother's number before she reached the end of Garrett's driveway.

"Good morning, Mother. How are you on this fine morning?" Frankie's perkiness gave Peggy pause.

"I'm well, Dear. Thank you for asking. You're calling awfully early. Now, what's up?" Her skepticism couldn't be disguised.

"You'll never believe what I found," the excitement rose in Frankie's voice, and she didn't bother waiting for a reply. "A sleigh—a real horse-drawn sleigh. But . . ." her voice broke off when Peggy gave an excited wow on the other end.

"As I was saying, Mom, it needs some work, maybe a lot of work. We aren't sure, but Garrett promises he's going to find someone to check the mechanics. It may or may not be roadworthy by the festival." Despite her uncertainty, Frankie sounded more upbeat than usual.

"Who's this Garrett you speak of?"

Frankie filled her mother in with the small amount she knew, making sure to specify that she had found his dog, the only reason she was at his house.

"Okay, Francine. I'm not interrogating you. This is an exciting development. I hope it works out for the Holly-Days. Please keep me posted." Did Peggy mean the sleigh or the coroner, Frankie wondered.

Frankie could picture her mother crossing off an item on her task list, maybe two items in this case: one for the sleigh and one for finding her daughter a suitable man. List-making was a habit she passed down to her daughter, who had a list going all the time, sometimes three or four.

"Have you heard from Violet? When will she be home for Christmas?" Peggy asked about her introverted granddaughter, a sophomore, who was still adjusting to college life after a drama-filled first year.

"I just sent her a final exam care package loaded with bakery. She's working on final projects this week, and exams begin the week after next. She'll be coming home on the 22nd." Frankie added "call Violet" to her to-do list.

"Oh, by the way, Mom, did you stop by yesterday afternoon and fix a broken tree-topper I had sitting on the bar?"

Peggy emphatically denied having any knowledge about the angel tree topper. Frankie couldn't argue with her mother. For as long as she'd known Peggy Champagne, she never knew her to lie to anyone about anything. So, the mystery remained unsolved, since nobody else but Carmen had a key to the shop. Frankie had unlocked the door after returning from church, so she knew the place had been buttoned up, and she had no security cameras to tell the story either. Her conversation, however, ended happily with Peggy's offer to work any extra shifts her daughter needed.

Frankie parked the SUV in the city's plowed lot across from the bakery, rather than navigating the alleyway, but she walked down the alley anyway, just in case she might see a red-hatted sprite. She knew better than to press her luck as she'd already been led to the sleigh by some force of nature that morning.

Frankie glowed from the inside-out as she bounded up the back steps into the bustling Bubble and Bake kitchen. She waltzed right into a concert of Jovie, Chloe, Sharmaine, and Carmen tapping, humming, whistling, and singing merrily along to holiday tunes on the local radio station. Frankie found herself joining in, dancing around to hang up her coat and tie on an apron as the aroma of fresh baked goods bounced about the room.

All four exchanged knowing looks, but Carmen didn't waste any time asking about Frankie's trip to Garrett's house.

Frankie filled them in on Garrett's house renovations first, building up to the discovery of the horse-drawn sleigh and the plan to make it operational for Holly-Days.

Carmen smiled at her friend with a hint of sarcasm. "So, your glowing face is all about finding a sleigh, huh?" Then Carmen ducked out of the kitchen with a fresh carafe of coffee to take out front before Frankie could shush her.

Everyone was posted at a station working on cookie orders, so Frankie scooted to an empty kitchen corner, determined to work on Christmas kringles. She had rolled out butter and dough into sheets the day before, and they were waiting in the walk-in cooler. She began cooking a large kettle of custard as a base for the special fillings she only made for holidays. The custard, combined with cranberries or pumpkin or chocolate, filled the kringles that disappeared from the bakery as quickly as they were packaged.

Once the Christmas kringles were made, Frankie could concentrate on butterhorn orders as the next taxing endeavor. By Christmas, her whole crew would need a spa day for their aching arms, necks, and shoulders. She was just thinking about which baker she should teach to make butterhorns when Carmen peeked around one swinging cafe door and motioned for Frankie to come over.

"What is it?" Frankie noticed Carmen's wide eyes and crooked grin.

"Someone's asking for you. And he's handsome, too." Carmen gave Frankie a little shove toward the front counter. She noticed Garrett Iverson, pleasantly peeking at the pastry case. He looked up as soon as he saw movement.

"Hello again, Frankie. I thought I'd better stop by and test out your wares before they're gone," he said, good-naturedly. "Besides, I want to give you an update on our secret mission." Garrett winked.

Frankie greeted him cheerfully, and recommended the morning rolls, kringle wedges, and apple crisp danishes with the robust Foglifter Blend coffee. As she packed his purchases in a box, Garrett gave her the news on the sleigh.

"I had a brainstorm and visited the Amish village south of town after you left. Harley Yoder and his sons are coming over tomorrow morning to look at it. Provided, that is, if you're willing to pick them up." Garrett presented his poker face.

"What do you mean, if *I'm* willing to pick them up?" Frankie was guarded.

Garrett laughed and held up both hands. "Well, there's four of them, Miss Francine, and they won't all fit in my truck, so I was hoping you'd follow me out there, since, you know, this was your idea." There was no annoyance or anger in his voice.

Frankie backed down. "Sure, I'll follow you out. What time tomorrow?"

"How's seven work for you?"

Frankie hesitated. The shop opened at 6:30 a.m. and Saturdays were the busiest days in the bakery. How many items were on her to-do list for tomorrow?

"Seven works great. Right, Frankie?" Carmen interrupted Frankie's mind jumble.

"Sure." Frankie waved at Garrett's goodbye-and-see-you-tomorrow.

"Don't worry, Frankie. We'll be fine here. Everyone's

coming in for the weekend to play catch-up, including your mother."

"That's the point, Carmen. I should be here working, not running around Amish country to fix up an old sleigh," Frankie tsked at her friend.

Thinking about the sleigh reminded Frankie that she still needed to connect with Bob Dugan, the owner of Snowy Ridge Christmas trees and annual provider of the mammoth town tree.

"Hey, Bob, this is Frankie Champagne from Bubble and Bake. I'm just checking to see that all is ready for delivering the town tree to Spurgeon Park before next week?"

"Yep. The tree is being cut today; in fact, we're heading over there shortly. She's a beauty, Douglas fir, 40 feet or so. I expect she'll be hanging off the trailer when we load her up." Bob was alternating between chewing some sort of breakfast item and gulping a beverage. Snowy Ridge's busy season was in full swing from November until mid December. The company provided tree lots with cut evergreens from Milwaukee southward to Orlando, Florida.

Frankie tapped her pen on the yellow notepad. She jotted down "Douglas fir, 40 feet, cut today," although she wasn't sure she actually needed the information. "I'll check with public works to be sure they have the equipment your crew needs when you bring it into town, later today?" It was a question since Frankie wasn't sure when the tree was being delivered or exactly what constituted the equipment provided on the city's end.

"Um-hum," Bob began. "Not much of a crew really. It's usually just me, my foreman JJ, and Ted. Ted gets the hoist, lift, and flood lights. That pretty much takes care of it. We'll bring it into town later today or tomorrow after work."

"Ok, well thanks, Bob. Always great to have a tree from your farm." Frankie meant it sincerely. Snowy Ridge had delivered two trees to the White House in its 30-year tenure, bringing tremendous pride to Deep Lakes.

Frankie herself had worked at the tree farm on the topping crew one high school summer. Her job was to shape the topmost tree branches into the traditional tapered peak where the star or angel would proudly perch. Frankie remembered climbing some of the taller trees in order to crop the tops and coming home from the heat of summer coated in sticky pine sap. Still, she made good money for a teenager, and her co-workers were a fun group.

The phone conversation with Bob didn't provide much solace to Frankie, who kept an ironclad schedule. She didn't know if she was supposed to remind Ted about the equipment or rely on Ted and Bob to sort it out. And, she wasn't sure if the tree would be delivered today or tomorrow. When did Phil say the fire department would be stringing the lights and placing the famous star on top? Furthermore, was it her job to be worried about the details at all?

Fate had plans of its own that Friday, however. By mid-afternoon, snow was falling at a heavy clip. The fat flakes, clustering as they fell, piled up quickly. Every baker in the shop was immersed in a project, so nobody seemed to notice the accumulating snow. Around 3, Frankie's phone jarred her out of her fixation with kringle fillings.

"Oh hey, Mom—What do you mean are we going to open the wine lounge? Why wouldn't we?" Frankie looked out the window, rapped on the counter to get the women's attention, and pointed outside. They all gathered around the window, jaws dropped. Snow was falling sideways, swirling around at random intervals in various directions.

"Don't come in, Mom. We'll handle it from here. I'm thinking nobody will be out and about tonight. I'll talk to you tomorrow." Frankie hung up, told Carmen she should go, then turned to Chloe and Sharmaine.

"I think you two should spend the night here. I don't want you out on the roads, and we need you tomorrow. What do you say?" Frankie spoke matter-of-factly. Chloe and Sharmaine looked at one another, shrugged and nodded.

"I've got two empty bedrooms upstairs and extra clothes. We're all set." She looked over at Jovie. "What do you want to do, Jovie? I'm sure your mother expects you to be home by 5?"

Jovie nodded, reluctantly. "But, I'll get us shoveled out early in the morning and head in here right afterwards," she promised. Frankie was happy to count on Jovie, but understood the situation was a two-way street: Jovie didn't want to be home with her overbearing mother.

Carmen patted Jovie's arm. "I'll pick you up in the morning. It's on my way. Let's say six?" Jovie's house wasn't exactly on Carmen's way, but she suspected her mother wouldn't give Jovie a hard time if someone from the shop picked her up for work.

"I just heard from the boys. The school loaded up the buses a little early to get the kids home by dark. They're walking down here, so we'll head out when they get here."

Frankie was relieved that Carmen wouldn't be alone traveling the back roads to the farm.

"At least tomorrow's Saturday, so school won't have to be cancelled again. If this weather keeps up, we'll be going to school until July!" Carmen predicted. "But, at least we have able-bodied shovelers on hand," she enthused.

When Carlos and Kyle arrived, they decided to do a round of shoveling to try to stay ahead of the storm while Frankie and Carmen mass-produced several flatbread pizzas for the hungry crew plus two.

Sitting around the kitchen merrily eating, it was agreed that Frankie, Chloe, and Sharmaine would burn the midnight oil to fill orders, prep pastry dough, and bake more sheets of gingerbread. Carmen and Jovie would arrive by six, at the latest, to pick up where the others left off. Nobody could predict what kind of Saturday the tricky weather would deliver.

Carmen was just about to leave when her phone

buzzed. Her husband, Ryan, was on the line with news that made Carmen shudder. She reclosed the back door and sat down at the counter.

"The Snowy Ridge delivery truck is missing. Ryan said the tree was supposed to be here at 2 o'clock." The women looked at the kitchen clock. It was 5 p.m. "The last anyone heard from Bob and JJ was at noon. I guess the town is organizing a search."

"I'm calling Alonzo," Frankie said impulsively but then set her phone down, realizing the sheriff would be bearing the brunt of coordinating the search. She drummed her fingers noisily on the counter, perturbed. "Who can we call to find out what's going on and what we can do to help?"

With Alonzo tied up, Mayor Adele and the city council chairman absent from town, who would know what was happening? An idea pinged in Frankie's mind, and without dwelling on it, she tapped in Garrett's number.

"Hello, Frankie. Everything okay?" Garrett asked. His voice had an edge to it that Frankie hadn't heard before. The thought that Garrett had Frankie's number in his contact list registered briefly.

"I'm sorry to bother you, but we heard about the Snowy Ridge truck, and were wondering what we can do to help, or if there's any news?"

"Sure, sure. Alonzo is coordinating search crews using the county plows that are out clearing the roads. But he's also rounded up some of the firemen and others who have big trucks with plows attached. Problem is, they really don't know exactly where to look. Bob's wife can't confirm which field the tree was being cut from, and they've got fields all over the county."

"Thanks, Garrett. It sounds like the searchers have their work cut out for them. Wish them luck."

Frankie felt helpless and restless. "We have to do something. I know we can't go out looking, but there must be something we can do."

"Maybe we need a prayer vigil. That's what my family in Mexico would do—just gather everyone together to pray." Carmen raised worried eyes. "I know Ryan is taking his truck out to look. We all know someone who's out there searching, Frankie."

"I'll call Father Donnelly and my mother. If anyone can muster a prayer brigade, it's Peggy Champagne." Frankie smiled with the satisfaction of having some purpose.

Carmen knew Alice Carson, the Methodist minister, so she placed a call to her at the same time. Chloe, Sharmaine, and the twins were amazed at how quickly the two shop owners managed to rally four local churches and the city clerk to initiate a vigil at the community center. Peggy Champagne, armed with her contacts directory, started a phone chain to spread the word. Chloe chimed in that a social media post about the vigil would reach a lot of people quickly, too.

Frankie and Carmen's hygge environment at Bubble and Bake served a new purpose: the two boxed up every battery-operated candle in the shop to take to the center. Frankie raided the freezer, too, bringing bakery that wasn't designated for someone's order.

Carmen smiled, "Gotta feed the body along with the soul, huh?"

"It can't hurt, right?" Frankie donned her heavy parka and headed out to the SUV where Chloe and Sharmaine waited. The two had cleared snow off the vehicles while the twins shoveled another path. Snow continued to fall relentlessly, and the wind seemed to be blowing harder. They all looked at each other wordlessly, thinking the same thought. *How would the searchers be able to find anyone in the whiteout, in the darkness?*

Chapter Nine

The Bubble and Bake group met city clerk, Kelley LeVay, unlocking the community room door. Each one laden down with boxes of baked goods and candles, Kelley directed them to a front table she'd covered with a cloth from the kitchen.

"Dixie from the diner is bringing coffee. The ministers are on their way in." Kelley seemed calm and prepared, instilling confidence. "Let's just put the candles on the front table, too. Guys…" she looked at Carlos and Kyle, "can you set up some chairs on that side of the room for those who can't stand?" The twins flew into action.

People began streaming into the community room; some quite somberly, others chatting about anything they could to help ease the tension. Chloe spied a bewildered-looking Jovie scanning the room from the side doorway and went to gather her into their sector. Bob's and JJ's wives arrived together, hands clasped, worry on their faces. They were greeted with hugs and hand squeezes.

The ministers, dressed in regular street clothes, clustered together at the front of the room, and took turns leading prayers. This continued for about a half hour, followed by a cappella singing of "Amazing Grace,"

"Comfort My People," and other hymns. Then, silence consumed the room.

Nobody wanted to leave, waiting for news about Bob and JJ. Everyone took solace in the bakery and coffee, making circles around the room for whispered small talk. Several business owners approached Frankie to apologize for their poor behavior the night before at the planning meeting.

"Rob and I and several others on the parade committee contacted everyone on the list to invite them to ride in the parade again this year, Frankie," Sandy from Holiday Stationstore said. "We got together this afternoon to get the job done. We all felt bad about not being organized last night. Just wanted you to know."

It seemed that a snowy Friday in Deep Lakes was more productive than ever as many committee members checked in with Frankie to share their progress in finalizing event details. Whatever the reason for the fully charged committees, Frankie was grateful and relieved; she still felt responsible for the success or failure of the holiday season in town.

Across the room, she caught a glimpse of Jewel standing next to Father Donnelly, offering him a cup of coffee. She wanted to thank Jewel for the idea of bringing the committees together, and to let her know things were working out. Then she remembered why they were gathered here, hoping the Snowy Ridge crew would be found safe and sound. She inwardly berated herself for thinking about the festival plans when so many of the town's loved ones were in harm's way in the snowstorm.

Frankie headed in Jewel's direction when she was interrupted by her sister-in-law Shauna, who had brushed up against her side. Shauna was pale and looked tired.

"Is James out looking, too?" Frankie guessed. James had a heavy-duty truck with a plow he used as the construction company truck.

Shauna nodded. "Yes. They're all out in teams of two, searching in tandem, just to be safe. James has the coroner with him, and they're following Alonzo and Troy Larson, who are in one of the county plows."

Frankie was relieved that James was with other capable men, but her heart skipped a beat when Shauna mentioned Garrett.

"Don't worry about Alonzo. He's in good hands, Frankie." Shauna gave Frankie's arm a squeeze, then moved on.

Naturally, Shauna must have read the worry on Frankie's face and assumed it was meant for Alonzo. Now was not the time for Frankie to ponder her feelings.

Frankie continued across the room to Father Donnelly but noticed that Jewel wasn't in sight. The priest smiled amiably at Frankie, shook her hand, and introduced her to his niece and nephew.

"This is Aline Andrews, my brother Tom's daughter, and her husband, Mike Andrews."

"We stopped in last week to visit for a couple of days

on our way up to Hayward for Mike's family's gathering. Guess we're meant to be stuck here," Aline poked the priest playfully with her elbow. "Sorry, Uncle Patrick. You know we love visiting you." Then, returning to the somber topic of the day, she added, "I do hope they find those men safe and sound."

Mike and Aline shared some background information with Frankie but were interrupted when a small hand tugged on Frankie's sleeve. Frankie looked down into the cherubic face of a little girl with light blonde hair and expressive blue eyes.

"Oh, hello there. And who might you be?" Frankie asked.

"This is our daughter, Natalie. I don't think she knows what to make of all this," Aline gestured at the crowded community room, dimly lit with people in various emotional vignettes.

Frankie knelt down to talk to the little girl. She remembered all too painfully when she'd had to explain adult situations to her own daughters, particularly after their father left and moved to Wyoming. Those thoughts, combined with the present situation, brought Frankie to the brink of tears.

Reaching for Frankie's hand, Natalie spoke first. "I know everyone here was praying for the men out in the snowstorm, but I was praying for something else." Natalie's eyes were wide and sorrowful, looking deeply and honestly into Frankie's.

"And what were you praying for, Natalie, if I may ask?"

One tear slipped down the little girl's cheek. "For my kitty to be found. I lost her, and she's out in the snowstorm, too." Her little voice wavered, breaking a piece of Frankie's heart.

"Oh sweety, I'm so sorry about your kitty. Did you lose it today?"

"No, a long time ago. But I miss her. Do you think Santa will think I'm naughty and not bring me any presents?" Natalie was as sober as a judge with her question.

Aline jumped in with explanations before Frankie could respond. "Natalie lost her kitten a few days ago, right after we arrived in town. The kitty was a birthday present last month, and Mike and I told her what a big responsibility it is to be a caretaker for a pet. She took that to heart you see, so she's been distraught since Frosty disappeared."

Trying to absorb the information, Frankie put herself in the little girl's shoes. "You know, Natalie, I think Santa will know you're trying your best to be a good girl. When I was around your age, my parents told me Santa was going to bring me sticks and coal for Christmas. I guess I wasn't a very good girl that year. Well, when I opened one of my presents Christmas morning, the first thing I saw were big sticks. At least, that's what I thought. They turned out to be the legs of a standing chalkboard. Santa knew how much I liked to play school. But, when I thought I was getting sticks for Christmas, I tried even harder to be good afterwards."

Natalie's eyes grew as large as saucers as the story unfolded, and she breathed an audible sigh when Frankie wrapped it up. Carmen, who showed up in time to hear the tale, looked at Frankie in wonder.

"Is that story true, Frankie?" Carmen whispered.

Frankie nodded, replying, "Mostly. I know it's hard to believe, but I could be a little dickens sometimes." Frankie winked at her friend.

Out loud she said, "Carmen, can you please take Natalie to pick out a cookie?" Then Frankie turned her attention to Aline, and pulled out her phone to show her a photo of Cookie Cat. "Aline, is this Natalie's kitten? I found her behind the shop a few days ago."

Aline gasped. "I think so. I mean, it sure looks just like Frosty." She squinted to view the photo with more scrutiny.

"If Frosty is a Norweigian Forest Cat and about three to four months old, this is probably her. I took her to the vet, who told me the breed and age. Anyway, come by the shop on your way back to Father's and have a look." Frankie handed Aline a slip of paper with the address. "I'm going to head out soon and wait for news there."

Frankie was getting restless, and she wasn't alone. Having milled around the room, the hundred or so others looked ready to give up waiting and return home. The ministers appeared to notice the collective restlessness at the same time.

Father Donnelly spoke first. "If any of you care to

gather at St. Anthony's tonight, I plan to open up the church." Pastors Schinkel, Carson, Rawlins, and Hammond added their churches to the announcement, and people quickly dispersed afterwards.

Frankie and her crew, plus the twins, returned to Bubble and Bake and scattered among the Scandinavian-designed furniture around the lounge, each lost in their own thoughts. A little later, a sharp rap on the shop door brought Frankie out of her worry. She looked up to see Aline, and waved her to come in.

The door opened, allowing a spurt of snow to enter with Aline, whose dark blonde hair was covered in wet flakes. It seemed as if the sky didn't know how to cease its wailing barrage.

"Mike and Natalie are in the car. I didn't want her to come in, you know, in case it's not Frosty. I just can't bear to see her heart broken again." Aline looked ready to cry.

While Carmen talked to Aline, Frankie ran up the stairs to retrieve the sleeping kitty from her apartment. Aline's face lit up in joyful recognition.

"Oh, Frosty, you little rascal. It's so good to see you!" Aline scooped the kitten into her arms. Frosty yawned, stretched, arched her back, and mewed softly as if nothing new had happened. "Here, Frankie. Can you take Frosty while I get Natalie?"

Frankie smiled, buried her face momentarily into the cat's thick fur and listened to her loud motoring purr. "I'll miss you, Cookie Cat," she whispered, secretly.

Natalie danced in pure delight when she saw Frosty, her hat nearly falling off her silky blonde head. "Oh, Frosty, you're safe! I missed you; don't ever run away again." Natalie held the kitten gently. Frankie was thrilled and surprised to see Natalie and the cat meet, head to head, gazing into each other's eyes like kindred spirits. Frosty meowed low, rubbing her face against Natalie's cheek. It was precious.

"Thank you, Frankie. I guess it was meant to be that we saw each other at the vigil tonight. There's one answered prayer, for sure. I hope we get another one soon," Aline said.

Natalie hugged Frankie tightly, thanked her, and left, holding Aline's hand. "We'll stop in this week before we leave, if it ever stops snowing," Aline said on her way out.

Frankie locked the door, invited everyone upstairs, and turned the shop lights off, except for the Christmas lights. Carmen considered going home with the boys, but even the boys suggested the drive would be more challenging than it was worth.

Frankie showed Chloe and Sharmaine the two extra bedrooms where they would sleep, then rummaged through clothes to find something comfy for each one to wear to bed. Baking would have to wait until morning, since concentration was next to impossible. The two interns seemed ready for sleep anyway, figuring they could start early tomorrow; they set an alarm for 3 a.m.

Frankie handed the TV remote to the boys, and

they lounged on the couch, laughing at some late night cartoon teens love to watch. Carmen and Frankie sat at the kitchen table, trying to distract one another with contrived small talk.

"So, now you're back to an empty nest, Frankie. You lost your menagerie in a day," Carmen said through a yawn. She sat with her hands folded on the table, tapping her feet on the floor in an agitated pattern. Frankie reached over and covered Carmen's hands with one of her own.

"It's going to turn out okay, Carmen. And you know that Ryan will be safe. He's got a super-duty truck and lots of winter driving under his belt."

"Yeah, I know, but I just wish he'd call or something. I mean, we haven't heard anything from anybody," Carmen whined, then tried to cheerfully change the topic. "So, when does Violet come home from college?"

"Oh, Violet. She'll be home on the 22nd. Will and Libby are bringing her, and then we'll have a family celebration on Christmas Eve day at my mother's." The mention of Violet brought a furrow to Frankie's brow.

Knowing Violet had a tough freshman year of college and almost didn't return to Stevens Point last fall, Carmen was concerned. "Is everything okay with Violet this semester?"

"School is going better this semester for her. But, when I talked to her today, she was feeling doubtful about singing at St. Anthony's Christmas Eve service."

Carmen and Frankie were both members of the

church, and Frankie sang in the choir. Violet had been singing every year at the Christmas Eve mass since middle school, but the tradition always brought out the rivalry between her daughter and Tara Mabry. Tara had a clear, lovely voice and always sang a number of solos on Christmas Eve, to Violet's dismay. Frankie's introverted daughter could belt out a song in good old-fashioned gospel style, but since she was shy, she was frequently overlooked for solos. The same had been true throughout the girls' school years. Both Violet and Tara were in high school theater, but Tara always received the part Violet wanted, even though both auditioned. Tara's bubbly personality won the day, in spite of the fact that Violet may have been the better songstress. After six years, nothing had changed—the rivalry lived on.

"Violet needs to learn to stand up for what she wants, Frankie. I don't see why the choir can't split up the solo parts." Carmen had always been assertive, something Frankie herself struggled with well into her adult years.

"You are absolutely right, Carmie, and I'm going to tell Violet that when she gets home. The only problem is that Tara already knows the songs, and her grandmother is in charge of the music," Frankie reminded her.

Carmen wrinkled her nose in mild disgust. "Oh, yes. Rose Mabry and her old-maid sister, Dorie. Every year we have to listen to the same music, done the same way, by the same people. You should say something to Steve— he is the choir director, after all."

Frankie pushed back on her friend. "Maybe you should say something to Steve. You're not in choir, so he might listen to you. Coming from the choir, it sounds like a complaint. Coming from the congregation, it's a suggestion." Frankie made air quotes around the word *suggestion*.

Both women laughed, temporarily forgetting the snowstorm and lost Christmas tree truck. Both were jolted back to reality when their phones rang simultaneously. Ryan was calling Carmen, and Garrett Iverson was calling Frankie.

* * *

After checking fields 13, 14 and 15, Team One turned off Fawn Avenue onto Evergreen Lane, another snowdrifted road. Lon and Troy led the brigade in one of the new double-winged county plows, followed by James and Garrett within visual distance, but just barely. The search teams numbered six, communicated by radio, and were in contact with dispatch for storm updates and other emergencies, should they arise. Two county ambulances, parked and running with EMTs ready, were waiting at the sheriff's department.

Carmen's husband, Ryan, and one of the local firemen ended up joining Team One, after a quick decision was made to resurrect Old Yeller out of retirement. The cumbersome yellow road grater/digger/snow plow hadn't been in normal operation for a couple of years, having been replaced by newer, faster plows. But Old Yeller had the capacity to drive through the worst storm—albeit at a snail's pace. Eventually it became impossible to find parts to maintain the engine, so it was parked permanently in the back of the county garage until tonight, when it was called out on a quest to navigate the treacherous snowstorm to rescue Bob and JJ.

Ryan used to drive the yellow dragon. He worked part-time for the county on the night shift when the winter weather called upon his services. But when the behemoth was retired to the county garage, Ryan decided it was a good time to end his part-time gig. Since Carmen was running the shop with Frankie, Ryan could concentrate solely on sheep farming.

Bob's wife, Ginny, gave maps to the search crews, the fields with the tallest trees circled in red. The teams divided up the fields by area, knowing it was going to be a long night navigating the roads in slow motion, trying to stay sharp-eyed in the darkness. Each crew had night-vision goggles, but since there weren't enough for everyone to have a pair, they had to move at an even slower pace.

Field 16 was about three miles down Evergreen, but the men would swear it was ten or more, such was the pace. By now, searchers were getting punchy: some talked about everyday events in an attempt to lighten the mood, while others were silent, lost in their own thoughts. The heavy-falling snow lit by the headlights became hypnotic, making it difficult to focus, even more difficult to see anything beyond the squall.

Lon, who had been sitting slump-shouldered, suddenly sat up straighter, sniffing the air like a bloodhound. Troy looked warily over at his partner, waiting silently for Lon to speak.

"You smell that?" Lon picked up his radio and held it to his mouth at the same time.

Ever the smart alec, Troy managed a short snort. "Why, did you let one go, Sheriff?"

James answered the radio chatter. "Copy that; the coroner and I smell something sweet, too—like bakery?" The words came out a question of uncertainty and disbelief.

Ryan was next to pick up the discussion. "Hey, Lon and Troy. Look straight up ahead of you. We're looking at lights—kind of radiating, like a searchlight maybe?"

"Huh? Where are you looking, Ryan?" Lon spoke sharply. He was weary and fearful for everyone under his watch.

"About ten o'clock," Ryan confirmed.

Off to the left, the shoulder dipped sharply into a ditch. There were no reflector posts to be seen, no mailboxes, no houses. This could be the location of field 16, or it could be someone's hunting land, for all they knew.

Troy chirped through the radio static. "I smell it now—almost smells like sugar cookies."

Alonzo was worried about their mental state. Could they be hallucinating? High stress situations could certainly produce hallucinations, but he'd never heard of people smelling things that weren't real. Then, he spotted the lights off to Troy's left. He expected to see lights that quivered or pulsated like strange swamp gas or even the Northern Lights, but these lights were beams, as if from a high-powered, large searchlight. The beams pointed downward on the left, beyond the deep ditch.

"Wait, we need to stop. I see something!" Garrett said, excitedly. Looking through infrared binoculars, he saw a small red shape in the expanse beyond the ditch. "Nine o'clock, past the ditch about 20 feet or so, there's some kind of life."

The brigade slowed to a cautious stop. Lon looked where Garrett pointed, and he saw the red shape, too. The area was populated by white-tailed deer, so Lon wasn't too hopeful about the sighting. Troy had his own night scope with him, and he used it to scan the perimeter of the scene.

"Hey, I think I see a piece of a truck. Just beyond the red thing. It's covered with snow, but it looks like the cab right there," Troy said, matter-of-factly.

All of the men looked hard, wanting to see what Troy saw. James and Ryan caught a snatch of metal reflecting off the beams, which seemed to burn more brightly once the search party halted.

"I see it too," Ryan said. James affirmed as well.

"Okay, the question is: how are we supposed to get down there? Anybody see a driveway?" Lon was trying to be practical for safety's sake, but inside, his heart pounded, and he was jumping out of his skin to get out and search the field.

Ryan pulled up alongside the lead plow with Old Yeller, then carefully crawled ahead of the plow to turn the monster's headlights sharply ahead toward the left, seeking a driveway. The bright beams landed on a post with a red reflector, barely visible above the deep snow.

"There, see it? The post—that's got to be the driveway!" Ryan sounded hopeful.

Lon quickly reined in his team. "Okay, here's how this is going to go. Ryan, pull ahead and off to the right. Grab a lantern and hold onto each other as you head down. Stay together. James and Garrett: park behind Ryan, also on the right. Grab your lantern and meet us down there. Troy and I are going to try to pull into the driveway, just enough to shine down into the field, and hopefully not enough to get stuck."

Lon instructed Troy to give it a go with the plow. The driveway was just about the width of a tractor, so the plow had about enough room, but it had to back out to drop the double blade, an impossible maneuver on the narrow roadway. Somehow, after three tries and some fancy piloting, Troy wielded the plow into the driveway, made a small swath to pass through, and parked, engine idling.

He and Lon grabbed flashlights and the first aid kit, and scrambled down from the tall plow, leaping like white-tailed deer over the ditch toward the truck. Looking back at the others right behind him, Lon pointed toward the light beams and mysterious hump in the field. The others made their way toward Lon when the searchlight beams disappeared.

The team didn't have time to register the strange phenomenon, as they ran head-on into the Snowy Ridge flatbed, lying on its side, mostly covered in fresh snow. Using the piled snow like a ladder, Troy and Lon made a strenuous climb onto the driver's side door, shined lanterns inside the cab, and spotted two men. JJ was in the driver's seat, raising one hand weakly to acknowledge the searchers.

The door was stuck shut, perhaps frozen or maybe damaged from the accident. James had a pry bar with him from the construction truck, and Garrett was carrying a bolt cutter. Lon signaled to JJ to try to roll down the window, but either JJ couldn't or the window was stuck. JJ shook his head and pointed to his right arm, grimacing in pain.

Lon shouted above the wind, "Okay, JJ, brace yourself. We're going to break the window. Turn away and cover up."

JJ nodded, and Lon broke through the glass with the pry bar handle. Lon used utility scissors to cut JJ 's seatbelt, then hoisted him out of the truck and into the arms of Troy, who carried him as swiftly as the deep snow allowed to James' truck, laid him on the back seat of the king cab, and wrapped him in a warming blanket.

"Looks like you got banged up some," Troy said, checking over JJ carefully.

JJ barely nodded, but managed a short reply. "I think my arm's broken."

Troy stayed with JJ and, per instructions from Lon, radioed dispatch with the news.

Meanwhile, Garrett, smaller and more limber than Lon, scrambled into the cab to examine Bob. Bob was semi-conscious and appeared to have a head injury. Dried blood was caked on his forehead and crown, but he managed to nod his head in response to basic questions.

"Should we get dispatch to call an ambulance?" James asked. Garrett and Lon exchanged meaningful looks and moved off to talk alone.

"It's going to take too long for an ambulance to get here is my guess," Ryan said to James. "I think they're going to risk taking the men to the hospital themselves."

"Garrett's a former medical examiner, so he can make that determination after checking them over," James said. "Besides, we already moved JJ, so it's too late to change that protocol."

Lon and Garrett returned, announcing they would get Bob out and skip the ambulance. "Garrett's going to check Bob's vital signs, and then we're going," Lon said.

"James, can you and Troy take JJ to the hospital? Troy's a first responder, so if you don't mind driving, he can ride in the back with JJ." James nodded and headed to his truck, but Lon called him back.

"I'm going to have Ryan take the yellow dragon down Evergreen where it meets 3rd Avenue, then out to WH, then Riverside. That's going to have to be the best route to the hospital," Lon explained. "Garrett and I will be right behind you."

Garrett had Bob by that time and, with James' help, was sliding him onto the seat of the truck cab. Lon climbed in, scrunched himself into the far corner of the driver's side, and watched Garrett squat down on the floor of the passenger side, acting as a shield for Bob's prone figure.

Led by the slow but steady moves of Old Yeller, the unlikely parade plodded through the path made manageable by Ryan. They arrived at Laura Ross Wolcott Memorial Hospital in about 20 minutes. Emergency staff met them in the parking lot with gurneys and a round of applause. Ginny Dugan and JJ's wife, Annie, burst from their vehicle at the same time and trailed behind the ER staff.

* * *

After Carmen and Frankie finished their respective phone conversations, they hugged, then exchanged details shared by Ryan and Garrett. Neither of the women could contain their tears of relief that it appeared all would be well.

"Did Garrett say anything to you about the strange

light beams that led them to the field, then disappeared?" Carmen's voice had a skeptical edge.

Frankie nodded, eyes wide in contemplation of the possible divine intervention. "Did Ryan say anything to you about the sweet scent they smelled before they saw the searchlights?"

"No, he didn't. But you can bet I'm going to ask him—maybe tomorrow, after I give that man a giant hug!" Carmen gushed. "I'm going to get these boys home to bed. Thank goodness tomorrow is Saturday."

"Sleep in, Carmen. I've got lots of help here in the bakery. You come in whenever you can, and if you can't make it in, don't worry about it. I'll call Jovie to let her know." Frankie suspected yet another slow day of sales was on the horizon. Still, she, Chloe, and Sharmaine could get cookies ready for pick-up. Next week would bring an avalanche of orders to fulfill.

Chapter Ten

A sharp rapping on the shop door jolted Frankie off the kitchen stool she'd been resting on the past few minutes. She turned to look at the wall clock. It read 6:30 a.m. Frankie, Chloe and Sharmaine had been in the Bubble and Bake kitchen since 3:30, trying to get a handle on holiday orders. The short night's sleep had taken its toll on the trio. Sharmaine's head, held up by her hand, was bobbing as she read social media posts on her cell, and Chloe had dozed off at the counter, her forehead resting on an oven mitt. They barely registered the knocking noise.

"Oh gee, it's 6:30 already. I guess we better open up. Someone's looking for bakery!" Frankie trotted out the swinging door to the front. She half-expected to see Jewel waiting at the door, but the handsome face of Garrett beamed through the glass as he peered in.

Frankie smiled back and unbolted the lock.

"Good morning, Garrett. Good to see you," Frankie was still reeling from the events of last night and felt emotional seeing Garrett, who had been on the frontline of the rescue. "You're my first customer of the day."

Garrett stamped his boots on the mat. "Ah, good morning to you, too. But, I'm not here for baked goods, Frankie." She responded with a quizzical look. "Remember? We're going out to Harley Yoder's place to pick up him and his sons?"

Frankie had lost track of the date, what with the emergency situation of yesterday. "Oh dear, I forgot. You know, last night was a long night . . . and I'm so glad you found Bob and JJ. Well done," Frankie stumbled awkwardly, uncertain what to say, even more uncertain about her own emotions.

Garrett smiled at Frankie, eyes softened. "I'm glad everything turned out well, too. But, now, we've got a sleigh to fix, right? The Yoders will be expecting us—there's no way to reach them other than in person, so..."

Of course, the Amish community didn't use phones or technology of any sort, so they would assume today was business as usual, even with the snow storm. The plows had worked through the night and early morning to make the roads passable, so the two made ready for the drive.

"Why don't you sit a minute and help yourself to coffee and something from the pastry case while I get my car started," Frankie gestured toward the table and chairs in the front window. "Oh, everything will be out in a jiffy."

Frankie retrieved the pastry case, meeting Chloe after she emerged from the bathroom looking fresh-faced and perky in a bright red apron. Chloe wheeled out the coffee cart and began stacking coffee mugs by the carafes. She poured a cup for Garrett. Besides the usual regular and decaf, the shop offered Jingle Java as the flavor of the day, a brew from Door County Coffee. Chloe thought it would be yummy with a sticky bun, a.k.a. caramel pecan roll.

"Hey, Chloe. Garrett Iverson and I are heading to Amish country to pick up some men to look at a sleigh." Frankie told Chloe she'd fill her in later with details. "Can you and Sharmaine handle sales and clean up while I'm gone?" Chloe gave her boss a thumbs up.

Frankie headed back through the kitchen, donned her parka, and grabbed the snow shovel that was propped beside the back door so she could shovel her way down the steps. She gasped in surprise when she got to the last step as she saw a shoveled path to and around her SUV, which was also completely cleared of snow.

"Well, well, well. That coroner would be a good man to keep around, Francine," the Golden Firefly trilled in Frankie's ear. Frankie didn't mind Goldie's gratuitous comment for once. She started the SUV and looked down the alley out to Meriwether Street. The alley had been plowed as well. Garrett certainly had earned free pastries today.

Rather than tracking snow through the kitchen and shop, Frankie scampered down the alley to the street, and up the shop's front steps. Garrett was sitting by the window, two coffees in hand, chatting with none other than Jewel.

"Good morning, Jewel. I see you've met our county coroner," Frankie said cheerfully. "We've had some excitement in town. But, of course, you already knew that. I saw you last night at the prayer vigil," she recalled.

Jewel nodded, sipping hot chocolate. "Yes, but I came here hoping for some news, and I'm happy to hear it's good news."

"Hey, Frankie, if you're ready, we should get going. Might take awhile on the roads this morning," Garrett said and handed Frankie one of the coffees and a bakery bag with a Glorious Morning muffin inside—her favorite. "Good to meet you, Jewel." He nodded at the diminutive lady, who produced an impish smile.

The Amish community in Whitman County was several miles south of Deep Lakes on rural roads. In Wisconsin's other three seasons, Amish country was a tourist destination, populated by quilting shops, furniture stores, bakeries, greenhouses, and farm markets. But the winter season brought stagnant quiet, just as it did in much of rural Wisconsin.

The large white houses of the Amish were nearly lost in the deep snow—only made visible by the black buggies parked near the entrances. Several Amish children dressed in basic black waved at Garrett's hefty truck and Frankie's SUV as they passed by. The smaller children played joyfully in the snow mounds, while the older ones shoveled out paths and driveways.

The Yoder farm was a sprawling property with a carriage house, mammoth red barn, and other outbuildings. The wood-framed rectangular house rose two stories and sported an expansive chimney and open front porch.

When Garrett signaled to turn into the driveway, several young rosy-cheeked boys and girls, who had been shoveling snow, parted the way on two sides. They all smiled curiously at the visitors.

Harley Yoder, who was perhaps in his 50's, wore the typical wide-brimmed felt hat, which looked as weathered as his face. Here was a man used to hard work and long days outside in the sun and wind.

Harley shook hands with Garrett but merely nodded politely at Frankie. He spoke only what was necessary and no more in his interactions, not just with Garrett but with his own children as well. At his direction, the girls made a beeline back into the house to resume other daily activities. The smaller children went behind the house to play in the snow, while the middle-sized boys headed to the barn for chores. Three of the oldest boys came forward to meet Garrett, shook hands, and introduced themselves as Junior, Fletcher, and Eli.

Frankie hung back from the menfolk discussion, as seemed culturally appropriate. She was out of place here, and Garrett had to give reassurances that all would be well if two of the boys rode with her back to his place to look at the sleigh. Finally, Harley grunted his consent, loaded tools into the back of Garrett's F250, and grabbed Fletcher by the shoulder, pushing him toward the truck.

Since Junior was an adult and Eli barely a teenager,

their father had indicated both would ride in Frankie's
backseat, where Junior would be in charge of his younger
brother. Frankie backed out of the driveway first, leaving
room for Garrett to lead the way back to his place.

Frankie's attempt at friendly small talk was fruitless,
met only with bowed heads and polite nods by the boys,
who only spoke in their own dialect, if they spoke at all.
Frankie noticed that Junior, whose real name must have
been Harley too, was the only son with a beard. Eli was
still baby-faced, and she guessed that Fletcher was an
older teenager, and probably unmarried. She was sorry
that she hadn't thought to pack some baked goods to
offer them.

Once the group unloaded at Garrett's, chatter spurted
forth like a gusher among the men as they walked around
the sleigh, looked at its underbelly, and examined its
runners.

Garrett let Freya out for some exercise, and she made
herself at home in the barn, following the men around as
if she were part of the consulting crew. Eli climbed into
the driver's seat and grabbed the reins, making a remark
that brought forth raucous laughter. Frankie wasn't sure,
but she guessed the Amish were making fun of the
modern beings who wanted to make the sleigh usable for
impractical reasons, like pleasure. Freya jumped into the
seat beside Eli, hoping the sleigh was ready for a test ride.

The Yoders continued a loud, inscrutable conversation,
gesturing at different parts of the sleigh, making notes

in the air, and glancing at Frankie and Garrett like the foreigners they were. She and Garrett exchanged questioning looks, shrugged, and waited. Harley spoke with Garrett about the process of "fixing her up," as he put it, to make it driveable. The two men shook hands, then Garrett turned on the portable heaters in the barn so the Yoders could start working.

Garrett motioned for Frankie to come outside where the two could talk privately. Freya followed Frankie out of the barn, nuzzled up around her legs, and gently butted her furry head against Frankie's hip. She gave the dog some loving strokes, thinking the two were kindred spirits of some sort. The three of them stood in the sheltered area between the barn and shed, out of the wind, which had kicked up and begun blowing around the fresh snow.

"Well, what should I do to help? It doesn't look like the Yoders are excited about having a woman around," Frankie grumbled. She understood the Amish had different customs and practices, but she didn't like being looked down upon for being female.

Garrett noticed Frankie's dander was on the ascent. "Whoa, it's okay, Frankie. Beggars can't be choosers, remember? These guys know how to fix the sleigh, and that's what matters right now."

Frankie relaxed, looked down at the ground, and kicked at a snow drift. "Why don't I go back to town, then? Maybe we can work on the interior tomorrow, after church?"

Garrett looked pleased. "That's a good idea. I suspect they won't finish today. Depends on if they need parts to make the sleigh run. But, in the meantime, we can clean up the interior, and I'll look into getting some paint for the exterior. And, I'll poke around for some sandpaper to clean up the scrollwork between the bed and runners."

Frankie nodded and began walking toward her SUV, the elkhound on her heels. "Okay, I'll call you tomorrow before I come out." She bent down to whisper sweet praises in Freya's ear, who responded by licking Frankie's ungloved hand.

Chuckling, Garrett yelled at Frankie's back: "Are you coming back later to help me get the Yoders back home again?"

Frankie had already forgotten that the men would need a ride, and Garrett's truck couldn't hold them all. "Sure thing, Garrett. Call me when they're ready." She waved. Garrett smiled and said something, but his comment was silenced by the wind.

* * *

Back at Bubble and Bake, Carmen and Jovie were busy in the kitchen, whipping up yeast donuts, scones and muffins for Sunday morning. Chloe and Sharmaine had trekked home to Madison, and would return on Wednesday or sooner, if need be. Normally, the shop didn't open Sunday until noon for wine lounge customers, but Carmen decided that people would want sweet treats after church, since they were stuck with snow cleanup this morning.

"We can post online that we're open tomorrow. Church will be out by nine, so we can hightail it down here and open up right afterwards" Carmen suggested, and Frankie agreed.

"How did it go with Garrett and the Amish?"

An exasperated sigh escaped Frankie's lips. "Hmmm. The Amish men were not impressed that a woman came to pick them up. I don't think the father was even going to let me drive the boys until Garrett assured him it would be okay."

"Well, you know in their society, women have their place," Carmen reminded her friend.

"Yeah, I know. They made that clear. But, I think they were making fun of me and Garrett about fixing the sleigh. They were speaking in dialect, but whatever they were saying, they kept looking at us, gesturing, and laughing. At least we managed to brighten their day," Frankie giggled.

Changing the subject, Frankie asked if there was any news about Bob and JJ.

Carmen nodded emphatically. "I heard that JJ broke his collarbone, and Bob suffered a concussion from hitting his head when the truck tipped over. But, both will be fine—what a relief, no?"

Frankie grabbed some chilled cheesy-lemon scone dough from the cooler, and began rolling it out and cutting it into circles. Working with dough always soothed Frankie, no matter what life threw her direction. Baking always transported her back to her childhood, learning from Grandma Sophie in her old-fashioned kitchen where the blue and white Danish plates looked down on the two of them from the kitchen walls.

"Oh, I forgot the best part, Frankie," Carmen broke into Frankie's reminiscence. "Ryan says some volunteers went out this morning to dig out the truck and rescue the Christmas tree!"

Carmen explained that another Snowy Ridge driver would be meeting the volunteers, moving the tree onto a flatbed, and bringing it into town to the park today. "So, I guess it should be ready for the lighting ceremony Friday after all!"

Jovie produced a little clap. "I guess all's well that ends well," she pronounced. Despite Jovie's gloomy home life, she always found the silver lining in every dark cloud. Frankie was grateful to have her around.

The trio continued their work into the afternoon, wrapping up just before Garrett called Frankie at 3 o'clock to retrieve the Amish men. "They need to be back by sundown, since it's Saturday, and they have to stop all work to prepare for Sunday," Garrett told Frankie.

The progress report on the sleigh was positive. Most of the work was accomplished except that a new axle was needed just to be on the safe side. Harley Yoder said he could repair the old axle but wouldn't guarantee it would hold, so Garrett told him to order one from Schuman's Carriage Shop. Harley said they would be able to return Wednesday if Garrett could pick them up again. Harley emphasized that he and his son, Junior, could complete the sleigh work, so they would only need one vehicle on Wednesday. Frankie tried not to make too much of Harley Yoder's statement.

Garrett found paint for the exterior and upholstery cleaner for the velvet seats, so all was ready for his and Frankie's part, but they would have to wait until after the Yoders were done with the repair work first.

The delay was a blessing since Frankie would be needed at the shop after church Sunday. She still hadn't mastered how to be in two places at the same time, but she was working on it.

Her stomach knotted, however, at the realization the sleigh was needed by Friday, and she wondered just when she and Garrett, with their full-time jobs, would be able to get the sleigh spruced up. *Guess we'll be working after hours, by candlelight, just like the old days.* Frankie laughed as she could hear her grandparents' voices echoing in her mind.

"What's so funny?" Garrett brought Frankie back to the present.

"Oh, nothing important, just thinking about how much the world has changed since our grandparents needed horses and sleighs to get around. Sometimes, I think it hasn't changed for the better, either," Frankie concluded.

"Well then, Miss Francine, maybe a sleigh ride is just what the doctor ordered," he smiled. "By the way, I wanted to ask you about Jewel. Where in the world did she come from anyway?"

Frankie explained what she knew about Jewel's arrival on the train and how she didn't seem to be in a hurry to leave town. "Jewel marches to a different drumbeat than the rest of us with the holiday hustle and bustle."

Garrett paused in thought, as if delving into some unreachable place. "Something bothers me about Jewel, though . . ."

Frankie snorted skeptically. "That tiny lady? Hah! She's like a walking billboard for the true meaning of Christmas. Why, she even smells like Christmas!"

"That's it!" Garrett said with rising zeal. "She smells like custard or egg nog."

Frankie agreed.

"But, the strange thing about that is . . . well, we all smelled that very scent right before we found the Snowy Ridge truck."

Chapter Eleven

The next few days passed quickly as everyone in town fluttered around like individual snowflakes, each landing where needed to prepare for the holiday.

Sunday brought oodles of customers to Bubble and Bake who were itching to be out and about after so many snowstorms. The pastry case was empty by 11 a.m., and there would be nothing left to offer in the wine lounge except the usual savory fare. Frankie thanked Carmen for the great idea to open early.

"Oh, that wasn't my idea. Jewel suggested it. She said she overheard people saying they'd planned to stop by the bakery Saturday until the weather ruined their plans. They said they wanted goodies for Sunday get-togethers."

Frankie pursed her lips, feeling little cracks as she did so. Her mother often harped at her about lotioning her hands and applying lip balm. Uppermost in her mind now, however, was the wonderment of Jewel, the whimsical little lady who always seemed to deliver the goods for her, and maybe even for the town. *What was Jewel all about anyway? And how come nobody had seen Forrest yet?*

Customers told Frankie and Carmen that other businesses had broken their tradition of closing Sunday and, instead, opened for anxious shoppers who wanted to do some Christmas browsing and buying. Frankie smiled slyly at her business partner, one brow arched.

"I just wonder if Jewel influenced the whole town into opening their doors today," she mused.

Carmen folded her arms and stamped one foot. "Oh come on now, Frankie. Your brain is working overtime." She wheeled the empty pastry case into the kitchen, Frankie right behind her with empty plates and coffee cups. "I mean, I suppose she could have made suggestions. But, that doesn't mean anything, right?"

Frankie jumped on Carmen's hesitant response. "See, you're thinking the same thing I am, Carmie. What if Jewel was meant to be here for some reason?"

Carmen tied on an apron to do some cleanup before afternoon customers arrived for wine tastings. She offered Frankie eye rolls. "Yeah, what reason is that?" Her arms were crossed again.

Frankie's eyes came to life, ready to meet the challenge of Carmen's skepticism. "Oh, maybe like the Ghost of Christmas Present—here to teach us a lesson about the true meaning of Christmas?" Frankie spoke in her best theatrical voice, but her heart competed with her teasing remark.

Carmen released a skeptical groan. "You and your Scandinavian superstitions. They're almost as bad as my abuela's stories of the chaneque or Ryan's grandmother prattling on about leprechauns."

Carmen's next remark was interrupted by a rattling

sound against the back door. Frankie jumped and gave a little squeal. She dashed to the back door, opened it wide, peered around both sides of the deck, and came back in shivering and shaking her head.

"No idea, Carmen. There's nothing there," she pronounced.

"Hmm, maybe it was a bird or a branch," Carmen remained practical.

"It wasn't a branch. There aren't any trees close enough to the deck. I didn't see any birds flying around or eating at the feeders either. Maybe . . . it was one of the chaneque," Frankie finished, pouncing upon Carmen, making her drop the broom.

Thankfully, Carmen just laughed and gave her friend a little shove.

"Better straighten up before your mom gets here. You know she won't approve of your 'little people' ideas."

As if on cue, Peggy appeared through the swinging doors, dressed in a fashionable Christmas turtleneck tunic, black leggings, and leather ankle boots. She smiled sweetly at her daughter and gave her a small, tight hug.

"Thank you for calling me yesterday to let me know Bob and JJ were found safely. You know, I can't always count on your brothers to call. Sometimes I think they forget I'm alive."

Frankie was happy she wasn't on her mother's naughty list—a spot she too often occupied. This time she'd had the wherewithal to contact her mother instead of assuming she would hear the news from any number of people—which was usually the case.

Carmen said she would man the kitchen for the afternoon, filling orders for small plates of cheese and crackers, quiches, or flatbread pizzas. The women decided earlier to thaw out some frozen shortbread cookies and a couple of kringles to offer customers with a sweet tooth.

Frankie and Peggy each occupied one end of the long walnut bar, stationed with wine glasses and opened bottles, some chilled, some at room temperature. Pencils and tasting lists were ready for marking choices.

Most visitors were locals who came in to buy wine for gifts. Many of them did tastings to get reacquainted with the varieties, or to sample some of Frankie's new vintages since they'd last visited Bubble and Bake.

The Buzzards, a group of retired men who met weekly during the off-season at the wine lounge, occupied one corner. A lively game of Pinochle was in full swing; the men were happy to get together after missing last week due to snow. The Buzzards mostly drank beer, and helped themselves to free popcorn and half-price bakery leftovers from Saturday. Today, they grumbled some as there were no leftover goodies, so Frankie brought them some cookies, elbowing them to shush.

Except for the Buzzards, the shop was quiet, so Frankie joined Peggy on her end of the bar for a glass of Cupid's Cup, a seasonal variety that changed from year to year as it combined St. Pepin grapes with any leftover fruits of summer. Right now, Frankie decided a little taste of summer was in order, after the clobbering of snow the town received over the past week.

The mother-daughter pair sipped the fruity wine and stared out the window at the quiet street, still ruffled in snow around the lampposts with high ridges of snow on the curbsides. Each was lost in thought, caught up in a world that seemed to hold its breath.

Their reveries were interrupted by the jingling shop bell, announcing Natalie and her parents with Frosty in tow. The little girl had come to say goodbye and offer another thank you to Frankie for reuniting her with Frosty.

As Frankie bent down to pet the cat under the chin, Frosty turned, offering a tail swish in her face that made both Frankie and Natalie giggle.

"We're hoping to take home some of your delicious bakery," Aline said, looking around for the pastry case, which was now standing empty in the kitchen.

Frankie brightened. "You're in luck. I have two kringles in the back that I haven't cut into. One is cherry; the other is pumpkin custard."

"We'll take them both," Mike and Aline said at the same time, laughing.

The family was heading home, since their family gathering in Hayward would be rescheduled, hopefully before Christmas.

Natalie, looking angelic in her sky-blue bubble jacket

trimmed in white fluff, asked Frankie to tell her the story again of how she found Frosty. Frankie scooped up Natalie, with Frosty in her arms, and set her on a tall bar chair. She recounted the snowy morning, and the red bobbing hat on the tiny figure she saw trotting down the alleyway, who led her to the half-frozen furball.

"What's a nisse, Miss Frankie?" Natalie questioned, wide-eyed.

"Here, let me show you. You see, my dad carved nisser, among other creatures. His carvings live on the shelves around the lounge."

Frankie walked over to the bookshelf by the fireplace where her favorite vignette had been relocated to make room on the mantle for pine boughs and twinkle lights. The scene featured her favorite pair of nisser. The male had chestnut hair and beard, and was dressed in brown and green to blend with the forest. He held a bouquet of wildflowers behind his back for his girlfriend. The female nisse had long blonde braids tucked under her red cap. Her hands were folded in front of her blue apron with poinsettias on the pockets, and she wore a flirtatious smile beneath her apple-red cheeks. The two lived among driftwood, carved mushrooms, squirrels, and rabbits.

As Frankie drew near the shelf, all she saw were the animals sitting among the mushrooms—the nisser were nowhere to be found.

"I remember moving the whole scene here when we decorated for Christmas," Frankie said, perplexed. "Guess

I'll check with my helpers to see if they know where those little imps went. You just never know with nisser. They have their ways." Frankie arched her brows for Natalie's benefit and spoke in a mysterious whisper.

Then she proceeded to another shelf where two male nisser, garbed in blue pants and red pointed hats, congregated around a garden scene. "Anyway, here are two others." Frankie took one off the shelf and handed it to Natalie for examination.

"Oh, he looks like a garden gnome!" the little girl exclaimed gleefully. "Do you think the nisse led you to my kitty?" she asked.

Frankie speculated. "You just never know. But, I'd like to think so. They have a special bond with animals, after all. And, nisser can be good friends, if you're good to them. Since I was a little girl, every year on Christmas Eve we put out little wooden bowls filled with rice pudding to please the nisser, so they wouldn't play tricks on us the rest of the year."

Mike and Aline enjoyed hearing Frankie's tradition every bit as much as Natalie did. The two exchanged meaningful looks, and Mike explained: "Aline and I have been talking about making a special tradition for Christmas, and now seems like a good time to make that happen, before Natalie gets too old to believe in the magic."

Gazing at Natalie, then her parents, Frankie shook her head. "You're never too old to believe in magic, especially at Christmastime!" For the first time in years, Frankie was beginning to believe her own words.

She gave Natalie a warm hug, tapped her little nose, then buried her hand into Frosty's thick Norweigian cat fur. Frankie wondered if she should search for a Norweigian cat of her own, for she was smitten with Frosty and her wise, golden eyes.

*   *   *

Carmen and Frankie were alone in the shop kitchen Monday and Tuesday, kept on their toes by last-minute Christmas orders placed Sunday, Monday, and Tuesday by shoppers, who came out of the woodwork after the snowstorm. The partners decided to extend the ordering deadline, since the barrage of bad weather had waylaid many of their customers. It looked like cookies by the dozens, along with kringles and butterhorns, were the popular goodies that would be gracing many holiday tables around town.

Along with cookie and kringle dough, the two prepared giant tubs of icing for the gingerbread house contest, slated for Saturday. Frankie paused to assess the list of orders posted on the bulletin board.

"Two weeks, Carmie. You think we'll get all these orders filled in time?" The stress in Frankie's voice was evident.

"It's going to be okay. Every year since we've been

open, you get all worked up about the orders, but we always manage. And this year, we have Sharmaine to help out, too," Carmen reassured her partner.

"Of course you're right, as always. But, orders are up, so I just worry…" Carmen's response came in the form of a call to Jovie, asking if she would like to learn to make butterhorns. Since Jovie divided her time between Bubble and Bake and working at Shamrock Floral, Carmen wanted to be certain she had the extra time to work at the shop.

"I've been hoping to learn to make butterhorns," Jovie gushed. "The Healys need me for this weekend, but I can come in any evening or any weekday to help out." The upcoming weekend would be the busiest for both Christmas tree and Poinsettia sales at the florist's.

"There, that was easy. Jovie's on board for as much time as we need her, except for this weekend's Holly-Days festival," Carmen set her phone on the counter in a slam-dunk fashion.

Frankie felt better, also knowing that Chloe and Sharmaine would be there every day the rest of the week, starting on Wednesday. The two interns would be on hand to help with the gingerbread contest Saturday and said they would be there Sunday to work on orders, too.

And so, plans for the week were set and moving along like clockwork, even allowing Frankie time to check on the progress of the sleigh Wednesday after work. She drove out to Garrett's, and this time she noticed the winter white landscape reflecting off her headlights as she headed down County WH in the early evening darkness. She slowed down twice for deer on the shoulder, their heads bent down, scavenging for morsels of grain from the cornfields.

Garrett and Freya were stationed in the barn, Garrett sanding the metal scrollwork under the sleigh box, Freya lying down on the floor, watching his every move.

After exchanging hellos, Frankie put on household gloves that were sitting in a cardboard box with other project supplies. "So, did the Yoders finish their work?"

Garrett looked up from where he knelt beside the runners. "They did. So now the rest is up to us."

Frankie picked up upholstery spray to clean and freshen the dark velvet seat cushions. "You know, I'm skipping church choir rehearsal just for you," she teased.

"What do you mean, just for me, Miss Francine? I thought we were doing this for your mother and the community." Garrett tried to sound serious but was betrayed by his smile. "Well, I hope your choir director isn't too upset. You've got—what—two more weeks of practice before the Christmas service?"

A big rock landed in Frankie's stomach. Today was the 12th, meaning there was only one more choir rehearsal before the Christmas Eve service. A pang of guilt unleashed itself, spreading throughout her body. Why couldn't she be two people? There was that question again, plaguing her mind.

"Why can't you take on less—say *no* more often?" The Golden One stung Frankie's ears with her comment.

"Oh, shut up, for Pete's sake," Frankie said, aware she had spoken out loud when she saw Garrett's offended expression.

"Oh geez, I wasn't talking to you, Garett . . . I mean . . ." How was she supposed to explain away her comment? "I just realized there's only one more rehearsal before Christmas Eve, that's all, and I was feeling guilty." Her backwards explanation made Garrett laugh.

Trying to shake off her guilt and stress, she put all her effort into scrubbing the sleigh cushions, then grabbed a blow-dryer to hasten the cleaning process. A short time later, Frankie used the hand vacuum to suck up the dried shampoo residue. At least the noise from the blow-dryer and hand vac left zero opportunity for conversation, and Frankie hoped her awkward comments would be forgotten.

Garrett was done sanding the intricate metal scrolls by the time Frankie finished the interior cleaning.

"I think that's enough for tonight. Can you come by tomorrow, and we'll paint?" Garrett held up a small paint sprayer and metallic brass paint. "I'm going to use this for the scrollwork. Then, I'll polish up the runners and wax them."

He pointed to another can that contained exterior paint in dark red. "That's for the sled box," he said. "There's not too much to paint, so we should be done tomorrow, and the paint job should be dry enough by Friday night for sleigh rides!" He patted Frankie's arm reassuringly. "Don't worry, Frankie. We've got this."

Frankie was grateful. "Thank you so much, Garrett, you know, for doing all this. I mean, I kind of roped you into this project, and well, I appreciate it." Frankie swallowed a lump of emotion and a helping of pride that welled in her throat.

"Hey, if I didn't want to help, we wouldn't be doing this right now." Garrett gave her a stern look.

Frankie zipped up her coat and gave Freya a welcoming rub around her neck fur.

Well, thank you again, and good night. Oh, I almost forgot—what do I owe you—you know, for the sleigh repairs?"

Garrett waved his hand away in reply. "We'll discuss it later. Good night, Frankie. See you tomorrow at the same time?"

Frankie nodded. Suddenly, tomorrow seemed an eternity away.

* * *

Thursday dawned with a dark, threatening sky that made Frankie want to pull the blankets up higher around her neck and bury her face in her pillow. But, the glaring numbers on the clock were red eyes, probing her to get moving.

"Hi-ho, hi-ho, it's off to work I go," she sang in a

crackling morning voice, yawning in the middle. She looked in the mirror and cracked herself up.

"I don't see anything that amusing about your bed head, Francine," Goldie said sternly, which only made Frankie laugh again, especially when she fired her imaginary ray gun in Goldie's direction, making pew-pew sound effects. Goldie buzzed off to some netherworld.

A little later, Frankie was showered, outfitted in dark jeans and a tan turtleneck adorned with tiny pine boughs and reindeer, and bounded down her stairs, entering the shop kitchen in a flurry.

Carmen and Jovie were frosting fresh-baked pastries, and coffee was percolating. Carmen looked up suspiciously at Frankie's giddy antics.

"Looks like someone's having a good time fixing up a sleigh, eh, Jovie?" Carmen gestured toward Frankie with her head as both hands were busy icing cinnamon rolls. Jovie smiled warmly at Frankie, who made a sour face.

"I think I'm just over-tired. You know how I get…" she trailed off.

"Oh come on. It's nice to see you looking, well, stirred up, I guess. It's been a long time since I've seen that look on you. And it looks good, by the way," Carmen affirmed.

The truth was that Frankie didn't know how she felt, and didn't have the time right now to pause and examine any potential feelings she might have where Garrett was concerned. Changing the subject, she asked, "What's the featured pastry and coffee today?"

Jovie pointed to the cranberry-orange scones and salted pecan pastries with a flourish. Reading from the large packs of coffee, she announced: "White Christmas from Door County Coffee and Highlander Grogg from Beres Brothers."

Frankie gave two thumbs up. The shop vowed to carry coffees from Wisconsin roasters, and they were lucky to have several to choose from.

Jovie loaded the pastry case and volunteered to run bakery sales for the morning. Frankie and Carmen made a quick plan for the day and divided up the baking tasks among the five stations. Chloe and Sharmaine would be arriving any minute, and their stations were set with fresh aprons and cookie recipes.

"My mom will be here before four o'clock to run wine tastings and sales," Frankie reminded Carmen.

"Which reminds me—it's supposed to be your day off today, Frankie." Carmen brushed one index finger over the other in a shame-on-you gesture.

"You know I won't be taking a day off now until Christmas. That's why you came in yesterday, right—on your day off?" Frankie returned the gesture. "Besides, I'm not working all day. I'm going to be painting a sleigh by four o'clock." Frankie tossed the comment over her shoulder, then pushed the coffee cart out the swinging doors.

By late afternoon, light snow was falling, visible outside the open barn door at Garrett's. The heaters were going near the sleigh, but the door was opened to allow fresh air to come inside where Garrett and Frankie were painting. Frankie brushed the dark red paint on one side of the sleigh bed while Garrett carefully sprayed a second coat of brass paint over the scrollwork on the opposite side.

"What's the weather report?" Frankie asked, adding, "It's not looking too promising out there." As if acknowledging her remark, a gust of wind blew into the barn, carrying a flurry of snowflakes with it.

"I'm almost afraid to say it out loud, because you know that'll make it true," Garrett began, his voice muffled through the paint mask he wore. "We're supposed to get hit tonight with a doozy of a storm. It seems to be a pattern we're stuck in right now."

Frankie painted a little faster, then the pair swapped sides to proceed. The painting complete, Frankie lifted the drop cloth and plastic cover from the upholstery. The interior looked and smelled clean and refreshed. She stood back to admire their work. The brass scrollwork was dazzling, and the runners gleamed with polish and wax. The only thing out of place was the worn leather reins.

Garrett noticed Frankie's altered expression when she viewed the reins. "Oh, not to worry. I'm picking up new reins from the Yoders tomorrow morning. I'll replace these, and everything will be ready to go."

Frankie smiled. "Do you think the sleigh bed will need another coat of paint? I applied a pretty thick coat."

Garrett nodded, but told Frankie he would take care of the second coat tomorrow, too. "I have the day off, so it's not a problem," he added before she could protest.

By now Frankie was hungry, and snow was coming down harder and thicker. "I should get going before it gets any worse out there," she said, a little woefully. She had to admit to herself that she'd relished working on the sleigh with Garrett. After tonight, there was no reason for them to get together.

"Aren't you hungry, Frankie? I am. Maybe I could follow you into town, and we could grab a bar burger or something . . ." Garrett waited for Frankie to make the call.

"Okay," she said, trying not to sound too eager, but happy about the prospect.

It was a slow ride into town as the lines on the road were impossible to locate. Landmarks, too, were scarce—each large tree, empty field, or slope looked just like the last one. Disoriented, Frankie was surprised when town lights came into view, materializing out of nowhere. Garrett was still trailing her; the only two vehicles moving in the quiet landscape.

Frankie wondered if the Mud Puppy or Hat Trick would be open in this weather, but then remembered she was living in die-hard Wisconsin, where bars would stay open unless a court order shut them down. She turned onto Dodge Street and saw two trucks parked next to the Hat Trick. She pulled up behind the second truck and parked; Garrett pulled up behind her.

The burgers and fries tasted better than anything Frankie had eaten in awhile, and even though a Spotted Cow brew would have capped off the meal, both decided to forego alcohol, opting for Sprecher's root beer instead. They ate quickly, both thinking about driving back through the storm. Besides, Jimmy the bartender said he planned to close up as soon as they were done eating. He'd already cut off the three customers at the bar, serving them cokes or ginger ale, and making them sit at the bar another half hour before they could leave.

Still, Frankie and Garrett made small talk between bites, mostly Garrett, who shared details about growing up in Michigan, relocating to Wisconsin, and moving to Whitman County after being a long-term ME in Duluth and Superior.

Looking for a quieter pace, Garrett slowly migrated southward in the state, first to Green Bay, then to Deep Lakes to fill the vacated coroner post before being elected to a full term. Frankie didn't have an opportunity to ask why he left Green Bay, or if he was in a relationship or had ever been in one. The thought crossed her mind, but she received a sharp rasp in her ear from Goldie, so she pushed it out of her head.

Ever the gentleman, Garrett helped Frankie clear the rapidly accumulating snow off of her SUV before bidding her a good night. Since he was unwilling to take any money for the Amish repair work, Frankie insisted upon paying for supper, which he accepted. At the last minute she called out to Garrett as he climbed into his truck, "Could you please call me when you get home— you know, so I know you got there safely?" Garrett looked ready to make a snappy comeback, but just waved and nodded instead.

Frankie was already in her pajamas, curled up with a cozy Christmas mystery, when Garrett phoned to say he was home. At that moment, Frankie wished she either had Freya or Frosty for company. She made a mental note to call Dr. Sadie for another orphan as soon as feasible and then fell asleep, the book lying on her chest.

Chapter Twelve

Friday morning began with snow flurries. Frankie rose early to man the kitchen, guessing the poor weather would slow down everyone's attempt to get into town. She texted Chloe and Sharmaine at 4 a.m., telling them not to come until the roads were plowed. Carmen arrived around six with Carlos and Kyle armed with snow shovels. School was delayed until 10 a.m., so the boys once again provided the strength and energy for snow removal that the business partners appreciated.

Frankie was surprised to see so many people bustling about this early. She barely had the coffee and pastry cart in place before a stream of customers paraded in for goodies, tracking in a constant trail of slushy footprints. Nobody had time for small talk except to say they had things to do before the tree lighting ceremony and weekend Holly-Days. With everyone busily caught up in their own plans, they were oblivious about the looming demise of the Holly-Days weekend.

Ted Lennon hurried into Bubble and Bake, his city truck still running in a no-parking zone. "Morning, Frankie. I need a dozen of anything you got. Just mix 'em up."

"What's the rush, Ted?"

"I'm meeting some of the firemen up at the park, so we can get the lights and star up on the tree. We should at least be able to get the tree lit tonight, if nothing else," Ted looked expectantly out the window. "We've been trying to get up there all week, but this dang snow . . ."

"What's that supposed to mean? If nothing else . . ." Frankie asked.

"Well, rumor has it the ice sculptors have all bailed. And the parade performers, too."

Frankie blinked several times and pursed her lips uncomprehendingly. Finally, when Ted didn't explain, she asked why.

"We're supposed to get socked in here. Another storm is on the way, supposed to start cooking by noon. It's the one-two punch." Ted made a jabbing motion in the air.

Frankie couldn't believe her ears. After all the painstaking plans, delays, infighting, and near-tragedy, she couldn't conceive of the idea that the Holly-Days would not go on as slated. She quickly rang up Ted, then called Bonnie Fleisner.

"Fleisner's Hardware," a glum-sounding Bonnie picked up.

"Hi, Bonnie. It's Frankie Champagne. What's going on with the ice sculptors? I'm hearing rumors."

Bonnie moaned. "Well, they're probably true. One by one, the sculptors all called to say they were watching the weather. That was yesterday when they were already supposed to be here. As of this morning, they've all cancelled."

Before Frankie could react, Bonnie continued. "This is a disaster, Frankie. We're going to have to call off Holly-Days, and there goes the whole Christmas season. It's going to be a long winter. Sure wish the mayor was here—she'd know what to do." Then Bonnie hung up.

Frankie was mad enough to chew nails and spit rivets for more than one reason. Obviously, it was useless to be angry with the weather, since that was beyond anyone's control, but she hated it that the holiday plans for the town were falling apart. She hated it even more that Bonnie thought the mayor could save the day, implying that Frankie couldn't do the same. She had to think and decided that required additional caffeine.

Carmen found Frankie sitting in the lounge with a steaming latte, staring at the cold fireplace. She'd heard the news, too, and sat down beside her friend.

"I heard there won't be a parade or ice sculpting contest. I'm sorry. I know this event meant a lot to you, especially this year." Carmen told Frankie that school was closing right after lunch, even though it had started late. The boys were going to ride the bus home though, so Carmen was free to help at the shop the rest of the day.

"There must be something we can do to salvage a small part of the festival. I mean, the sleigh is ready, and there's plenty of snow. We could at least have sleigh rides tomorrow . . . and skating. We just need people to clear the rink. Everything's decorated at the park." Frankie's brain was cruising into overdrive.

"You're right," Carmen agreed. "We probably won't get out-of-towners here, but that doesn't mean we can't celebrate and have some fun. We can still have the gingerbread contest, too. Let's make some calls and spread the word."

The women made a list of people to contact, starting with Abe Arnold at *The Watch* and Kelley at City Hall. Carmen said she would get the twins to gather some friends to shovel off the ice rink tomorrow morning.

They both looked content until Frankie recalled how the parade was the highlight for the senior citizens in town. Not only would there be no parade, but she doubted many seniors would even come out for any of the holiday events, leaving them feeling isolated and disconnected.

Not one to throw in the towel, Frankie used the rest of the snowy afternoon to chase ideas around the empty shop, bouncing them off Carmen and Jovie, who escaped her mother before the heavy snow began falling.

The parade was supposed to begin at 7 p.m. and end at Spurgeon Park where the tree would be lit, followed by the Victorian-costumed carolers, and the youth ensemble from Madison. Putting their heads together, the three women concocted what they hoped would be a solution. If the ceremony and parade could be postponed until Saturday, their ideas just might work.

After a couple hours of writing notes, calling people

and texting others, Frankie said it was time for a much-needed break.

"Let's make pizzas—we'll save the quiches for the weekend wine loungers," she suggested.

Two large flatbread pizzas were baking in the oven when the back door opened to reveal Chloe and Sharmaine, each carrying an overnight bag. It was nearly 3 p.m., and Frankie and Carmen had figured their interns decided to wisely stay put in Madison.

"Dios Mío!" Carmen waved a finger at the two. "What are you doing here? You shouldn't have driven in the snow."

"We didn't expect you two, not in this weather," Frankie said. But, she felt a small pinch in her side—maybe from The Golden One—Frankie couldn't be sure. The pinch made her realize she needed to be grateful for her two bakers who felt dedicated enough to come to work, no matter the weather.

Frankie walked between the two, grabbed the overnight bags, and offered them seats at the counter. "Come over here you two, and we'll fill you in on new plans for the weekend. With the storm coming, we've been working non-stop on a Plan B for tomorrow."

"So, there won't be a parade or tree lighting tonight, then?" Chloe didn't sound surprised.

Frankie shook her head. "Right, and no ice sculpting contest either." She explained that with no sculptors, the event was called off. "We don't want to cancel everything though. I mean, people need to gather and celebrate, so here's what we're working on."

While Frankie explained and Carmen added in details from her list, Jovie cut the two pizzas into squares, passed out paper plates, and took orders for beverages. Chloe and Sharmaine relaxed into pizza-eating, enjoying some comfort after the nerve-wracking drive from Madison.

"Well, now that we're here, what can we do to help, too?" Sharmaine asked.

"Oh, there are still plenty of small details to take care of. But remember, if my mother shows up, please don't say a word. I want to try to surprise her if I can, and that's no small task." More than anything, Frankie wanted to prove to her mother that she could accomplish something important and make her proud. Moreover, she could do it without the help of Peggy Champagne.

Following her divorce, Frankie relied on both of her parents for help raising Sophie and Violet. After Rick left the family, she often felt like a rudderless boat, the wind knocked out of its sails. Her parents picked up the pieces in so many little ways, and although Frankie loved them for it, she wanted to stand on her own two feet. Once she landed a solid position as a paralegal at Dickens and Probst, Frankie felt more confident and able, knowing she could take care of her family by herself.

When Charlie Champagne died, Frankie was lost at sea once again. Her dad was both her confidant and her buddy; the two shared many of the same traits and interests. He was easy to talk to; she could be herself without judgment. For some reason, real or imagined, Frankie believed her mother scrutinized every decision she made, from the way she wore her hair to her career choices. Somehow, she believed she didn't measure up. So if she could succeed at pleasing her mother and helping the community—well, Frankie just needed a win.

Earlier, Frankie had heard from a historical society member that all of the musical groups had cancelled, stating they didn't want to chance travelling in the snow. Sharmaine, however, brightened a bit.

"Let me call my father. He has a beast of a Jeep, big enough to drive the whole ensemble here tomorrow. The roads should be better for sure, and I'm going to bet the ensemble doesn't have another gig tomorrow."

Frankie clapped, her face aglow. "If your dad and the kids' parents agree, you're officially my hero, Sharmaine! But . . ."

"We know, Frankie: we won't let your mother know," Carmen finished her friend's thought. "Let's just hope she doesn't have a backup plan of her own. I mean, you know your mother."

Oh yes, Frankie knew how resourceful Peggy was. But this time, Peggy didn't know the Holly-Days festival was still on, albeit a scaled-down version. Maybe by the time her mother discovered the new plan, she wouldn't have time to worry about scaring up new entertainment.

Besides, she'd still have the Victorian carolers, since most of them were locals.

* * *

Snow continued falling throughout the afternoon, heavy at times, then easing into sparse slivers before whirling back into motion again. Around five o'clock, Alonzo showed up at Bubble and Bake's back door, stamping his boots on the deck to announce his arrival. He opened the door enough to stick his head through.

"Hey, ladies," he said jovially, seemingly unfazed by the mounting snow. "I bumped into Nick, who said he'd haul his snowblower down here if he had a way," Alonzo began.

Frankie's brother, Nick, could be counted on to help out with any physical labor she needed.

"So, I brought my truck ramps over to his house, picked up the blower, loaded up my blower, too. Anyway, we're going to start moving snow. We'll come back tomorrow to take care of the rest." Alonzo tipped a two-finger salute to the women and shut the door.

Frankie ran to the door, opened it, and called down the steps after him. "You two are awesome! Stop in when you're done, and we'll hook you up with some grub." Frankie tried out a folksy bumpkin accent. Alonzo waved without turning around.

"That settles it, Frankie. I think we need to purchase

a snow blower of our own. At least, if this keeps up." Carmen was frugal but practical, too.

"Let's revisit the idea after the holidays. We can't spend the time or money on that right now." Frankie was thinking about their recent downward sales trend due to weather.

Amid the revving and humming of the two blowers, the women continued working on bakery orders, interrupted by community members who had questions and information about the new Holly-Days plans. About an hour later, Frankie and Carmen started assembling two more large pizzas, substantially loaded with meat and cheese.

When Nick and Alonzo showed up on the back deck, they looked like yetis. Frankie and Carmen had swept snow from the covered deck so the men could navigate easily and leave their boots behind. Frankie met them on the deck, broom in hand, and began brushing snow off of their outerwear.

Inside, brews were lined up on the countertop next to the cut pizzas. The men toasted the bakers, gobbled food, and headed back out to remove snow elsewhere.

"Hey, I heard about your ideas to have the holiday festival tomorrow. Good job, all. I'll spread the word," Alonzo grinned, high-fiving Frankie and Carmen. Nick echoed Alonzo's praise. Then they were off.

Ryan called Carmen and told her to stay put at Frankie's for the night. Visibility was poor, and the plows had been pulled off the roads until morning. It wasn't uncommon for Wisconsin counties to pull their plowing crews for the night on weekends. With most commuters done working for the day, counties chose to conserve their resources and their workers until the next morning.

By eight o'clock, the cooler was stocked with pastry and cookie dough, numerous cookie orders were stashed in the deep freeze, and the shop ovens were turned off for the night. "It's been a long day, and we've been superstars," Frankie said to the others, giving her feet a little air kick in celebration.

"We've got a huge day tomorrow, so let's hit the sack and reconvene early. How about 5 a.m.?" Frankie offered. The others agreed; everyone was exhausted, so the prospect of a lively all-girls slumber party at Frankie's was going to have to wait.

Chapter Thirteen

Frankie heard snow blowers and plows on the street before her tired feet hit the floor in her bedroom. "4:30 a.m., that's just about right," she said to nobody. Peering out the window like a small child, Frankie surveyed snow-covered Meriwether Street in the lamplight. She could see the plow had been out and back again as there were two swaths of cleared snow, and banks on both sides of the street. She heard a blower and wondered if Nick and Alonzo were at it already in front of the shop.

With four women in the house, one bathroom, and a huge day of running interference on gingerbread decorating, Frankie decided to take a fast shower right away. She emerged from the bathroom to find Carmen perking coffee in her kitchen.

"Next," Frankie giggled, waving her hand toward the bathroom, like a police officer directing traffic. "Are Chloe and Sharmaine awake?"

Carmen nodded and pointed to the living room where the two were sitting quietly in the dark, rubbing sleep out of their eyeballs.

Soon, everyone had showered and consumed their first java of the day. Daylight was still an hour or so away, but Carmen reported that she saw Nick and Alonso, along with other business owners, blowing snow up and down Meriwether and Granite streets.

"I guess that's the Deep Lakes parade for this year," she announced, laughing at her own joke. The others joined in.

"It's going to be a whole new kind of celebration this year, Carmen. I just hope it goes over." Frankie chewed on her index finger.

Downstairs, Chloe perked large carafes of coffee and hot water while Sharmaine helped Frankie set up tables for gingerbread construction, and Carmen brought sheets of gingerbread and icing out of the cooler to set up at the front table. Chloe loaded donuts, muffins, and scones into the pastry case and wheeled it out front, parking it off to one side. A self-serve beverage station perched next to the pastry case; a variety of tea bags and envelopes of hot chocolate hung out in baskets at the station. Later, plates of cookies would occupy both ends of the table.

Daylight eventually gave in, beginning with shrouded sunshine in thick cloud cover. The plows continued to maneuver around town in a repetitious path. Peggy Champagne arrived at the shop at eight o'clock through the back door.

"I see someone took care of clearing your snow, so I parked behind the shop. I want to save room for the festival-goers," Peggy enthused.

So, her mother knew about the new plan after all, Frankie surmised, but she wasn't about to add any details unless her mother provoked them out of her. Instead, Frankie decided to comment on the snow removal.

"Wasn't it great of Nick and Alonzo to clean up the snow? They started last night already and came back this morning. In fact, Carmen said many business owners were out early blowing snow on the main streets." Frankie felt a warm glow thinking about the community coming together to make the holiday fun happen.

"That was very good of them indeed." Peggy looked around the shop sitting area. "It looks like you had plenty of help this morning setting up. Maybe you don't need me." Her tone was expectant, inviting Frankie's response.

"Of course, you're needed, Mother. I'm hoping we'll be very busy today." Frankie wanted to reassure Peggy that, naturally, her daughter needed her help, even if she felt irritated with her at the same time.

A few local families showed up by 9 a.m. to begin designing gingerbread structures. As participants came in, Peggy wrote down their team names and members, assigned them table numbers, and showed them where to pick up supplies. Three long tables stood against the shop windows, two on the Meriwether and one on the Granite street sides for displaying the completed structures. Anyone was welcome to come into the shop and vote for their favorite structure, but the Bubble and Bake crew would judge the designs for their own awards.

All the tables were filled by 10 a.m., and the shop was buzzing with loud comments, laughter, and oohs-

and-aahs over the creative designs. A few people waited patiently by the pastry case for their chance to decorate. This pattern repeated itself throughout the day until the cutoff time of 2 p.m.

The gingerbread crafters navigated from other fun activities, including next door at Rachel's Bead Me, I'm Yours. There, the Knit Witches were helping people make yarn bells with jingling clappers for hanging on the town tree. Every bell had the initials or first name of its maker stitched on it.

Downtown, librarian Sue Pringle was posted at the senior center, busily pairing up eager senior citizens with children to cut out giant snowflakes, then decorate their original designs with glitter. Sue's capable assistants, Angie and Pam, organized snowflake making stations at the library and Sunny Ridge Senior Home, respectively. The idea was borne from a rendition of "The Twelve Days of Christmas" looping around Frankie's head—only this version was about the twelve snowfalls before Christmas.

Snowflake making supplies were easy to come by locally, and Sue and her assistants were happy to gather them and organize the event.

"What a lovely idea to get our seniors more involved in Holly-Days," Sue said. "Even better to pair them up with children. That's a win all the way around."

Frankie and Carmen had both felt disheartened, thinking about the disappointed seniors who looked forward to the annual Christmas parade. Many of them couldn't attend the ice sculpting or tree lighting, since they were outdoors, and getting around was difficult in the winter. But, the parade always circled the senior center lot and processed slowly past Sunny Ridge, so they had front row seats for it. The two were excited about finding ways to make the elderly the focal point for these Holly-Days and involve the whole community.

Judd and Bonnie Fleisner and other organizers of the ice sculpting contest were busy at the skating rink, directing concession providers to the wooden hut, and showing the pretzel guy and kettle corn guy where to park their operations. The rink was a hub of activity now that the ice sculpting contest had been replaced by a snow building contest. Families and kids of all ages turned out to play in the snow, which was perfect for packing. Around the perimeter of the rink, they built snow people and snow animals. Promptly at 4 p.m., their creations would be judged by the committee.

Best of all, the creations made that day would be featured in a reverse parade at the senior center. Volunteers from the parade committee set up queue lines in the spacious center's dining hall, wide enough for wheelchairs and walkers. Sue Pringle and library volunteers hung a ladder horizontally, using fishing line to dangle the handmade snowflakes at varying lengths. The effect was a whimsical indoor snow flurry.

The snow building contest committee set up a portable movie screen in another section of the parade line. Bonnie, for one, was grateful to have Kerby and Steffie Hahn in her charge after all. Both were techies who spent the day filming the stages of snow building from snowballs all the way to completed snow people and creatures. The two set up a projector at the senior center that ran a looping slideshow of the event, featuring kids and adults goofing off and showing off their creations.

Frankie, Carmen, and the rest of the Bubble and Bake crew slowly and cautiously carried the gingerbread structures out the front door of the shop to where Carmen's van and Frankie's SUV were parked. They loaded what would fit, moved the vehicles up the street, and loaded more gingerbread buildings into Jovie's minivan and the Healy's Shamrock Floral delivery truck. Glen and Meredith Healy, whose flower shop was just down the block, witnessed the laborious task and offered to lend a hand.

Thanks to Frankie's heads-up call to Sandy Nelson on the parade committee, long display tables were lined up along the mock parade route at the senior center. Sandy had taken the time to cover the tables with white cloths and cotton balls, which made the gingerbread buildings part of a snow-covered winter village. The winning structures were adorned with satin ribbons declaring them "most traditional," "most creative design," and "fan favorite."

Somehow everything was in place by 6 p.m. when the seniors would arrive, some transported there by the shuttle buses used during the summer for tours of the town. Stuart Ness, the Chamber chair, had actually come up with the idea to use the buses, taking a break from schmoozing the travel network to participate in the event.

"The buses are just sitting in the city garage. I don't think it would take much to get them going, and we'd only need a couple," Stuart suggested to Alonzo, the most official person he could think of to contact in the absence of city officials.

Alonzo said he could spare a few people and rallied Fire Captain Phil Mortensen to round up others. The volunteers met at the city garage to remove the chocks from the tires on the shuttles and to warm up the engines.

Other seniors arrived with family members or neighbors, many in wheelchairs or moseying along with walkers, footed canes, or on the arm of a loved one. Frankie and Carmen witnessed the gathering from behind the scenes, squeezing each other's hands.

"Look how everything came together! You did this, Frankie." Carmen whispered.

"No, we did it. All of us," Frankie murmured, a lump swelling in her throat.

The two women were behind a small staging area on one end of the dining hall that had been quickly crafted by the high school industrial tech and art departments. Miss Julia from Miss Julia's School of Dance agreed to bring her Snowflake Fairies Christmas program dancers to the center for a sneak peek of the upcoming show. Frankie and Carmen volunteered to help the dancers get into costumes, while Peggy, Chloe, and Jovie kept their eyes on the fragile gingerbreads. Sharmaine had sneaked off to Spurgeon Park to meet her dad and help organize the youth ensemble.

Frankie helped a little girl named Astoria into a dazzling white costume trimmed in what looked like a million diamonds. It took several minutes just to carefully pull up the skirt and fasten the delicate back material.

"Don't you look just like a snow princess!" Frankie exclaimed.

Astoria's face lit up, and she struck a pose. She handed Frankie a bejeweled tiara, elastic tie, and several bobby pins.

"I still need a bun in my hair though, please," the little girl said.

Frankie could barely manage her own hair, keeping it in a bobbed do that was easy to care for. Gaping at Astoria's long silky tresses, she felt daunted. "Ah, um, I think Miss Carmen would be happy to help you with your hair, Sweety." Frankie pointed to Carmen, who was finishing up a perfect hair braid on another dancer.

"Hey, Miss Frankie! Let's trade dancers. You can help with makeup." Carmen winked at her partner. Even though Carmen had two boys, she'd had plenty of hair practice on her sisters' heads. After raising two daughters, Frankie couldn't fathom why she never mastered hair management.

Makeup wasn't Frankie's forte either, but she figured she could create a passable result. Emberlynn, one of the younger dancers, pranced over to Frankie in her gold lamé costume, her dark braid bouncing as she moved. She looked every inch like a Christmas ornament. Emberlynn giggled as Frankie brushed metallic eye shadow on her lids and silver powder on her cheeks. She squirmed a little, causing a wisp of powder to float into her nose. Both Emberlynn and Frankie laughed as they sneezed at the same time.

A couple of the older dancers from the school arrived to expedite the costuming, hair, and makeup processes. Keeping the energetic dancers in tow was like wrangling a snowstorm, Frankie decided, conjuring memories of Sophie and Violet as little girls. Frankie had been a volunteer parent for numerous church plays and 4-H programs. Through the ages, it seemed little girls never changed.

At last, Frankie and Carmen emerged from backstage to join the parade-goers. The outdoor parade may have been called off, but the reverse parade was a big hit. Happy seniors and their loved ones meandered past the crafted originals, all made by local hands, all generating holiday cheer in abundance.

Before Miss Julia's dancers performed, contest winners were announced to loud acclaim by the audience. Frankie and Carmen presented a ribbon and bakery gift certificate to Juliana and Ali, sisters who designed the best traditional gingerbread cottage with a cookie wafer walkway, candy cane fence posts, and a gumdrop-studded roof.

Another set of sisters, Layla and Tesla, received the creativity award for crafting a gingerbread birdhouse with a pretzel stick roof and gold dragées for the siding. The two had made a bird nest from coconut with candy-coated almonds for eggs. Sitting on the nest was a gingerbread cardinal, iced in red. Frankie had a soft spot for birds, and she had a feeling the little girls knew it.

Finally, Carmen gave out the fan favorite award to brothers Zoren, Vox, Miro, and Oden, expert lego builders who transformed their lego savvy into building a gingerbread animal shelter with various cats, dogs, a couple of bunnies, and even a parrot. The boys managed to make their gingerbread look like lego blocks to boot.

Bonnie Fleisner took the stage after Frankie and Carmen, offering them each a genuine expansive smile. Frankie filed that smile away—could it be that the curmudgeon was softening around the edges?

Bonnie practically gushed, singing the praises of the Hahns for filming the snow builders and creating the slideshow at the center. Then, with assistance from Kerby and Steffie, she presented the awards for the best snow creatures. The top award for best in show went to Will, Kaleb, and Zed who crafted a giant Snow Wookie that made *Star Wars* fans cheer.

The seniors were treated to the Snowflake Fairies dance, and they exclaimed in delight at the beautiful spectacle as Astoria and Emberlynn twirled around the stage, accompanied by dancers waving jingle bells and colorful ribbons.

The finale came when the Victorian carolers took the

stage, sang three songs from their repertoire, and invited the seniors to sing along to "Silent Night" at the end. The song was a fitting culmination of holiday spirit, leaving many seniors teary-eyed.

The reverse parade had accomplished more than being a fair substitute for the traditional Holly-Days, and those in attendance were smitten with the Christmas spirit and feeling of community, unlike many past holidays. It was difficult to leave the tranquil senior center afterwards, but as chit-chat wound down, most people were anxious to venture off to Spurgeon Park for the tree lighting ceremony and outdoor festivities.

A procession of vehicles could be seen heading south on Granite Street, looking like a winding string of white Christmas lights gliding along the snowy pavement. The shuttles were out front as the drivers planned to park near the gazebo, allowing a front row seat for the seniors from Sunny Ridge.

The Bubble and Bake crew loaded into Carmen's van, which could carry eight passengers, and would return to the senior center afterwards for their vehicles. Even Frankie's mother rode in the van, singing praises of her daughter all the way to the park. Frankie tried not to get too full of herself, but she relished being in her mother's good graces.

"As I was saying, you certainly brought Deep Lakes together in a whole new way, my dear. Just wait 'til Adele Lundgren hears about this—she's going to think you're running for mayor. I mean . . ." Peggy cut herself short when the park gazebo came into view. She gasped.

The others looked first at her, worried if she was okay, then looked ahead where she pointed. The gazebo was alight, its columns wound with thousands of white lights. The town tree was lit in colorful lights, including the majestic 12-pointed star atop. The large oaks in the vicinity of the gazebo wore netted lights around their trunks in red and green. To everyone's surprise, a large lighted sign stood at the entrance in welcome, reading: "Merry Christmas from Deep Flakes!" They laughed at the clever play on words.

Frankie imagined there was a collective gasp as the moving trail entered the park. People nearly jumped from their vehicles, ran to the sign for a better look, and pointed at the tree and other lights. A few bounded up the gazebo steps to have a word with Fire Captain Phil, who had just arrived himself. Phil, who had been designated as emcee for the ceremony, was checking the sound system and looking around for the power switch.

Calm and steady, Phil was generally unruffled by disorderly situations. Such was not the case now as people attacked from all sides, asking him why the lights were already on.

"I just can't tell you why. I drove up here with everybody else, and the lights were all on," Phil sounded flustered. "I'll check with Ted Lennon. Maybe he knows something." But, Ted didn't know either. Nobody was about to take credit or blame for lighting up the park before the ceremony.

Phil regained composure and asked people to clear out of the gazebo and gather down below, so he could make an announcement. When Phil spoke, people listened.

"Good evening, and thank you for coming out to the park tonight. This is a special time for our community, as it is every year, during the holiday season. But, this year is more remarkable, not just because of Mother Nature's endless surprises, but because we came together as a community. We came together to find our friends, Bob and JJ. We came together to offer something special for families and our cherished senior citizens. We overcame adversity and created something memorable for years to come."

Phil's speech created a wave of pride that spread throughout the park as people applauded. He went on.

"Now I know we were supposed to have a formal tree lighting ceremony here. But wasn't it an awesome spectacle to see these beautiful lights as we were driving up the road, greeting all of us, like a Christmas card?" The crowd cheered.

"I agree," Phil said, clapping along. "Now, without further ado, let me introduce our special guests that braved the snowy roads to play for you tonight. Here are the Capital Youth Ensemble and Deep Lakes' very own Victorian carolers."

Peggy looked from Frankie to Sharmaine and back again when she saw the ensemble sitting on the gazebo stage. She smiled warmly at them, ready to listen to the music. The sextet featured 12 to 15 year-old musicians playing violin, viola, cello, French horn, trumpet, and saxophone. Sharmaine pointed out her brother Tyrel, serenely playing the cello, lost in the harmonious carols.

Deep Lakes seemed to be holding its breath. Not the slightest wind stirred. Not a single flake fell. The dark sky added to the park decorations, offering up a million twinkling stars for the view. Despite the clear sky, the temperature flaunted itself at 38 degrees, warm for a Wisconsin winter night.

After the crowd joined the carolers singing, "O Christmas Tree," a din of delight rose when the musicians pulled out sleigh bells, a slapstick, and temple blocks and launched into a rollicking version of "Sleigh Ride." The tune signaled the horses to pull up in the driveway, making the crowd ooh and aah.

Four draft horses from the Linde farm trotted into view first, pulling up into a wide spot of the parking lot for loading riders onto the hay wagon. Kids ran toward the hay wagon, stopped in their eager tracks by cautious parents.

More horses' hooves were heard cloppping in their direction, and everyone paused in wonder, waiting to see what was in store. Around the bend of the driveway, a team of horses, one black and one white, sprang from the shadows. Junior and Fletcher Yoder slowed the team to a halt, revealing the stunning Victorian sleigh with room for four adults or six children to settle onto its velvet cushions. Audible gasps could be heard throughout the throng, but Frankie only cared about one reaction in the crowd: her mother's.

Peggy closed in on Frankie, grabbing her arm. "Francine, did you know anything about this?" Peggy was flushed with surprise and excitement. Before Frankie could speak, Garrett was at her side, grinning.

"Not only did she know about it, Mrs. Champagne, she helped restore it to the spectacle you see before you!" Garrett bowed dramatically for effect, making Frankie giggle like a teenager.

Frankie knew her mother would want an immediate explanation, so she jumped in. "Mother, this is Garrett Iverson. I found his dog, you recall—the elkhound." Peggy nodded slightly, her brows still constricted into sharp points of uncertainty.

"Anyway," Frankie continued, "when I returned his dog, she ran off and we found her in the barn, and there was the sleigh—this is the sleigh I told you about," Frankie's voice rose in excitement, sharing the story. "I told Garrett that you and the historical society were looking for a sleigh to use for the festival. So, this has been our secret project for the past week. Garrett hired some Amish men and . . ."

"Never mind the details right now, Frankie. I want a sleigh ride." Peggy Champagne was not to be deterred. Garrett escorted her over to the sleigh where the Yoders were waiting for instructions. Fletcher held her hand, lifted her up into the seat, and waited for more arrivals. A queue formed quickly for the sleigh, but Garrett stood at the opening, waiting to lift Frankie into the seat beside her mother.

"I think you earned the first ride, Miss Francine," he said.

"No, I think *we* earned the first ride, Mr. Iverson," Frankie smiled. Garrett climbed into the seat behind Frankie and Peggy.

"Hey, Carmen! There's still room for you!" Frankie called out to her partner.

Carmen shook her head. "I'll wait and ride with Ryan and the boys," Carmen decided, gesturing behind her where the rest of her family was walking in her direction.

Frankie gave her the okay sign, and the Yoders hawed the horses into action. The ride around the park grounds was beautiful with the starlight and an almost-full moon shining like a glowing yellow beacon.

Peggy briefly grabbed her daughter's hand in hers. "I know you didn't do it by yourself, but you did a marvelous job of pulling all of this together. I mean it, Frankie. It's no small task to bring the town together with all its different personalities and whatnot." Peggy doled out praise like spices, sparingly. Frankie basked in her mother's approval.

The ride ended all too soon; the quiet of the parkway and the soothing horse steps were replaced by eager people excited for a sleigh ride. The hay wagon loaded up many youngsters and teens, anxious for a ride and too impatient to wait in a long line for the sleigh.

Garrett told Frankie the Yoders were willing to rent out their horses and their services for the next few Saturdays for more sleigh rides if the town wanted them. Frankie imagined the townsfolk would keep the Yoders busy.

"Maybe we started a new Deep Lakes tradition," Frankie gloated a little at the thought. She felt warm on the inside, thinking how the weekend had begun with dashed hopes for the Holly-Days, only to end with one of the best events in Deep Lakes' memory. Pride—that sometimes-saucy visitor—swelled in Frankie that night, perhaps in the whole community. Somehow, they had joined forces without their champion, Adele. Maybe, by some miracle, the Christmas Spirit had settled upon the entire town.

Chapter Fourteen

Although Frankie began the morning singing her heart out at St. Anthony's, the day felt a bit like a let-down after yesterday's crowning achievement. Following church service, Carmen and Peggy met her at Bubble and Bake to open the shop for after-church bakery before the afternoon wine tastings.

Frankie sent Chloe and Sharmaine home for some rest after last night's festivities, telling them she'd call if they were needed before Tuesday; otherwise they should get their own Christmas preparations underway while they had some free time.

Frankie wondered what had become of Jewel. She hadn't seen the little lady in a couple of days and, surprisingly, not at any of the Holly-Days events yesterday. She had never met nor even caught a glimpse of Forrest and wondered if he was even real. This notion reminded Frankie that she needed to ask about her missing carved nisser.

Neither Carmen nor Peggy knew anything about the nisser's location.

"Perhaps that visiting hound ate them, dear," Peggy offered, matter-of-factly.

While Frankie dismissed that idea, she proceeded to make another sweep of the lounge area, searching every nook and cranny for her favorite carvings. The tinkling shop bell brought her upright from underneath one of the coffee tables, bumping her shoulder on the corner as she rolled out. Frankie was reminded once again of her natural clumsiness. *My mother picked Grace as my middle name, but that didn't mean I received any,* Frankie always told people.

"Oh, Ms. Champagne, are you alright? I didn't mean to startle you." Frankie looked up into the angelic face of Tara Mabry.

"Oh, hello, Tara. I'm fine—I bump into things pretty often, so nothing new." Frankie was surprised to see Tara, who must be home from college, but truly didn't frequent Bubble and Bake. "Can I help you with something?"

"Well . . ." Tara began hesitantly. Her wide blue eyes gazed off, not meeting Frankie's. "I was wondering if you had a couple minutes? I want to tell you something."

Frankie led Tara toward a corner table and offered her a drink.

"No thank you. I'll pick up something to take with me when we're done," Tara said, now speaking with more conviction.

"I just wanted to tell you that I spoke with Violet on Friday, and I emailed her the musical pieces for the Christmas Eve program." Tara stopped, searching for words or maybe a reaction from Frankie.

Frankie knew Tara would be singing solos for the program, so she expected that Tara already had the music, since she was back in Deep Lakes. Of course, Violet sang in the program every year, too, so maybe Tara assumed that Violet was back from college, and she wanted to connect with her about the music.

"I know she won't be home for another week from school, but I wanted her to have the music so she could start practicing the solo parts." Tara looked down at the table when she spoke.

"The solo parts? I'm afraid I don't understand," Frankie said. "I mean, I assumed you would be doing the solos, Tara." Frankie's voice was cut with an unaccustomed shrillness.

Tara raised her dark glossy locks, showing Frankie her full face, which looked contrite. "That's what I'm trying to tell you, Ms. Champagne. I want Violet to do some of the solos. We talked, and I told her to pick the ones she wanted." Tara spoke easily now. "We're going to share the solo pieces this year. I know, it's about time, right?" Tara was feeding into Frankie's streaming thoughts.

Frankie was overjoyed for Violet but couldn't let Tara off the hook without further explanation. "I think that's wonderful, Tara, but I have to ask: why the change of heart? You and Violet always vied for the same solos and musical parts, and you always won them. So, why share them now?" That shrillness had crept back into Frankie's voice, making her feel ashamed.

Tara reddened. "I know. You're going to think I'm weird . . ." her voice trailed off.

Frankie had seen plenty of weirdness lately, why would another oddity rattle her? "Try me," she replied, firmly.

"I was at the library Friday, and I met someone. She kind of looked like an elf, a Christmas elf, except she had long blonde braids." Tara smiled, conjuring the image of the person who could only be Jewel, Frankie surmised.

"She was eating kringle, and that reminded me of your shop, which reminded me of Violet. We started chatting about all kinds of things, and she asked me what my plans were for the holidays and my college break. I told her how the Christmas Eve service was my favorite, especially singing the solo pieces."

Of course you did, Frankie thought, remembering that while Tara was the whole package of looks, smarts, and an angelic voice, she had a vain streak that caused her to butt heads with others since she managed to get her way most of the time. Frankie's unkind thoughts brought a smack from The Golden One above her ear.

"Go on," Frankie said, recovering.

Tara's pride dropped a notch as she continued her tale. "It was something she said—the elf lady, I mean. She told me that solos were enjoyable for the soloist, but a variety of voices created joy for everyone. She said we have to remember that sharing creates joy; if we keep everything good for ourselves, we steal happiness from others."

Frankie practically fell off her chair. For Tara Mabry to speak with such grace and maturity was astounding, and she had Jewel to thank for it. All the resentment from the past evaporated from Frankie's being. She scooted to the other side of the table and squeezed Tara hard.

"That was an amazing story, Tara, but what you did was even more amazing. You didn't have to act, but you did, and I'm sure Violet is thrilled." Tara nodded enthusiastically, unable to speak as tears slid down her cheeks.

"I'm so sorry that Violet and I wasted time being rivals when we could have shared the spotlight and had more fun," Tara confessed. "It's going to be good to see her. We made plans to get together to practice next week when she's home."

Tara rose, saying she had a lot to do at home before Christmas. Frankie asked her to wait, then wrapped up one of her special Christmas kringles in a waxed bag.

"Take this with you, and share it with your family, Tara. It's my special custard and cranberry kringle."

Frankie darted back to the kitchen to share the story with her mother and Carmen. Both were dumbstruck but grinned ear to ear. Peggy produced an uncustomary little "woot" in her granddaughter's honor.

"Well, I guess Jewel is still around, then." Carmen said. "Or, at least she was on Friday."

"Guess so," Frankie said, her brow furrowed. "I just don't remember her coming in to get kringle Friday morning, though."

Chapter Fifteen

Just about one week to go until Christmas, and it appeared Deep Lakes was making up for lost time due to the unprecedented December snowfall. Mother Nature smiled kindly upon the area and ushered in above-average temperatures and sunshine. The sunny days made for melting snow, which helped clear the back roads and downtown curbsides. Housebound Wisconsinites were itching to visit the unique small town shops that offered out-of-the-ordinary gifts to fulfill their wish lists.

Business was booming, and the cha-ching of cash registers could be heard above the Christmas bells around town. The horse-drawn sleigh rides attracted so many visitors that the Yoders added dates to their schedule. They offered weekday evening rides to customers hankering to grab a piece of bygone days. Even better, the local establishments stayed open evenings so folks had somewhere to shop, eat, and pass the time. Unknowingly, Garrett and Frankie, with the help of the Amish, had created a phenomenon.

Well before Christmas Eve, Bubble and Bake had sold out of all of its Winter Dreams and Hygge Holiday wines, along with a number of suitable substitutes. Frankie and

Carmen planned to reopen the winery earlier in January than originally slated to replenish supplies.

With the Bubble and Bake Christmas orders filled, Frankie and Carmen decided they would close after business on December 23rd until January 2nd to enjoy some family time. The shop would open today and tomorrow for product sales only. That way, Peggy could prepare for the holidays, and Chloe and Sharmaine could enjoy some downtime.

Frankie's daughter, Sophie, and her fiance, Max, would come for Christmas on the 24th. Since both worked as nurses at UW-Hospital in Madison, they were fortunate to be off Christmas Eve and Day. The two had worked extra shifts, including Thanksgiving, in order to secure the time off and would pull double shifts on New Year's Eve and Day, too.

Immersed in her own family traditions, Frankie hadn't seen Garrett Iverson since he stopped by to purchase wine the week after the tree lighting. She imagined he had a family of his own somewhere with plans on his calendar. Besides, she didn't want to dwell on Garrett right now— there would be time enough to do that after the holidays.

Nagging in Frankie's mind, however, was the little gnomelike Jewel. She couldn't believe Jewel would leave town without saying goodbye, but that must have been the case.

Jovie was ringing up wine sales out front, so Frankie was sorting through mail in the alcove of Bubble and

Bake, the quiet space she called her office. Violet would be home sometime that afternoon, and Frankie didn't want any distractions from their time together. So, with the shop closing next week for the holidays, Frankie figured she'd better face the mundane task of paying the monthly bills and reconciling her accounts.

She forced herself to complete the bookkeeping tasks before doing the most enjoyable act of the year: writing out Christmas bonus checks to the shop and vineyard crew. She left room at the bottom of the cards for Carmen to write a personal message to the workers, then wandered into the quiet Bubble and Bake kitchen.

The kitchen was dark; the absent hub of usual activity left an expansive silence and time for reflection. Frankie enjoyed a precious few minutes to think about December and its topsy-turvy mishaps and miracles. At least, Frankie viewed some of the events as miracles.

Maybe the biggest miracle of all was Frankie's change of heart toward Christmas. Things didn't have to be perfect for her to enjoy Christmas, and she had the most important reasons to be happy: her family, her friends, and successful businesses.

In the course of her musings, the back door swung open with a vigorous force that announced Violet, carrying a half-drowned orange-striped Tabby in her arms.

"Violet, what the . . ." Frankie began, befuddled by her youngest daughter ferrying in a cat.

"Quick, Mom! Can you grab a towel or blanket to

wrap this poor thing in?" Violet's jacket was dripping as she entered with the kitty, who appeared to be shell-shocked, but not enough to stop it from grumbling in low mutters.

Frankie dashed to the front lounge trunk where blankets were stored, made a pitstop in the laundry room for a dry towel, and wound back to the kitchen to hand Violet the towel first. Violet was cooing to the halfway-wet kitty and began rubbing its backside to dry off its fur.

"Explain, please," Frankie said, "and where's your luggage?"

"First things first. I was coming down the alley when I heard a ruckus by the creek. A cute little man was rescuing this cat. He'd fallen halfway into the water and was hanging on for dear life to the embankment. Anyway, when the little man saw me, he scooped up the kitty and jammed him into my arms. If you look out back, you can probably see him. He was trying to fish his hat out of the creek where it had fallen off..." Violet trailed off as Frankie threw open the back door like the kitchen was on fire.

Shivering, Frankie leaned over the deck, first looking toward the creek where she saw no activity. Then, a flash of red caught her eye, and she peered toward the alley, just in time to see the backside of a chestnut-headed elfin man in dark green pants, and high-top brown boots, carrying a dripping-wet red hat, and disappearing down the alley.

Frankie called after him but was answered only by the echo of tinkling laughter and sleigh bells. Muttering like the orange tabby, she came back inside. Violet wrapped the cat into the blanket while Frankie warmed some milk on the stove.

"Did you see him, Mom? The little man? He looks just like one of Grandpa Charlie's nisser!" Violet's declaration gave Frankie tingles.

"I just barely caught a glimpse. As for the nisser, boy do we have a lot of catching up to do, Sweety." Then she changed the subject to the cat at hand. "Let's try to get this critter warmed up, and then I'll give Dr. Sadie a call to see when she can check on him."

"Sounds good to me, Mom." Violet turned to nuzzle the cat's neck. "For now, I'm going to call you Forrest."

Frankie blinked, shivering again. "Forrest? Why, Forrest?"

Violet looked at her mother matter-of-factly. "Well, that was the little man's name. He told me his name, handed me the cat, and said the cat would be well-taken care of by the shop lady," Violet was struck by her mother's reaction. "Why, do you know Forrest, Mom?"

Frankie nodded her head yes, then shook her head no. She explained that she knew of Forrest, but she never actually met him. In fact, she often doubted he was real, since she'd neither met nor seen him in town. "Oh boy, here we go again." Violet's confusion would have to wait for further clarification until later.

Frankie and Violet relocated themselves and Forrest the cat upstairs where Frankie had a batch of Maple Bacon Chili in the Crock-Pot for supper. Thanks to

Violet's tech skills, Dr. Sadie video-chatted with the two, virtually examined the ginger kitty, and concluded that tomorrow morning would be soon enough to bring it in. *Good Old Dr. Sadie,* Frankie thought. *Of course she would come in Sunday morning to check on the cat.*

Later that night, the haunting whistle of a nearby train awakened Frankie. She ran to the window, looking out toward the train depot, all the while knowing she couldn't see that far in the darkness. She knew for certain she wasn't sleeping; the clatter of train tracks rumbled into the apartment, and her picture frames rattled on the wall.

A revelation struck Frankie just then, and she clambered down the stairs to the wine lounge. She ran to her shelf of woodland carvings, and there they were: the nisser were back again in their proper place. Was she seeing things, or did the little lady's eyes flash for a moment and her smile grow wider? Frankie couldn't keep from smiling as she peered upward at the angel atop the Christmas tree. "You know, don't you?" she said aloud to the angel. "But I guess you're not telling."

Frankie padded back to the shop kitchen where she rummaged in her apron pocket for the business card Jewel gave her the day they met. She fully expected it to have vanished just like her nisser. It was still there. Using her phone she punched in the number on the business card. A voice message said: "This is Jewel and Forrest. We are not available right now, but if you ever need us again, we're just a wish away."

Notes on magical creatures in

Deep Flakes Christmas: A Nisse Visit

Folktales, fables, myths, legends, fairy tales: I love every one of these literary genres. Growing up in a small town in the 1960's and 70's was a fortunate experience. The quiet, the lack of urban intrusion, modern conveniences, and material excess afforded me infinite hours to dream and imagine. And boy, could I imagine! I wanted to inhabit a world where fairies might live under the flowers in my backyard, where pixies might fly across the starry sky, and where the woodland critters might chat the night away at their own private party in one of our giant trees.

I remember repeatedly reading the mythology section of our Book Of Knowledge Encyclopedia starting when I was eight and continuing throughout my formative years. I colored in the glossy black and white depictions of the Greek gods and goddesses by giving them personalities and pretending they resided along the Fox River just below our house. I invented conversations and dances for them as I crashed their parties.

I gathered acorn tops and blossoms, leaving them in the mossy patches below the cottonwood and maple trees: adornments for the fairies to gather. I'm certain my older brother absconded with them, telling me he saw the fairies take them away. I wanted to believe there was magic in the world. I wanted to believe the sprites, even the tricksters, brought good fortune to the world, or at least taught us lessons about what happens to naughty children or anyone who messes with Nature.

My parents allowed us to imagine without censure— what a gift! My dad began carving nisses or nisser after he retired, but growing up we knew about gnomes, which we thought were just a Norweigian form of a dwarf (think *Snow White and the Seven…*). By the time I was in high school, Dad and Mom were making nisser in the Danish tradition, dressed in medium-blue, some sporting a pointed red hat, others wearing a light blue stocking cap. They even carved tiny wooden bowls with even tinier spoons so we could leave the traditional rice pudding—risengrød—for the nisse on Christmas Eve. Any house nisse who received risengrød reportedly would not play tricks during the year, but instead, bless the house with abundance.

In Scandinavian folklore, the nisser were in charge of the farmstead, especially the protection of the livestock. They lived in the barns and outbuildings on the farm, were typically solitary in nature, and thrived on order and cleanliness. If they were treated with respect, they brought success to the farm. Eventually, the domestic nisse evolved to be associated with Christmas and were known as the julenisse; jul meaning Christmas and nisse a derivative of Nicholas (think St. Nick).

Other Danish sources discuss the julenisser as a subculture of elves that live in forests, eat berries, and take up residence in houses during the Christmas season to make mischief. In Deep Flakes Christmas, my nisse characters combine everything I know and have read about the legendary little folk.

A note on cats: cats reportedly have special relationships with magical beings. Having extra-sensory perception, cats can detect the presence of spirits and will often make themselves scarce rather than endure the encounter. That's why the Bubble and Bake cat is never around when Jewel comes to the shop.

The Chaneque or Chanekeh are guardian sprites of Mexican folklore, originating with the Aztecs. Their name is from the Nahuatl word meaning "those who inhabit dangerous places." Like any figure passed down through storytelling, their characteristics vary. Their appearance is sometimes described as goblin-like, with large pointed ears and glowing red eyes, or as tiny children with old faces. They are depicted wearing straw hats and carrying grass bags for all their tricks. Sometimes they carry slingshots to shoot rocks at disagreeable humans! They are elemental forces in charge of fiercely protecting nature and bring woe to the individual who disrespects the natural world. The Chaneque were generally feared in many Mexican households because they were said to cause misfortune and accidents within the home. They are also accused of hypnotizing people into straying from home for days and forgetting anything that happened during their absence. Parents warned their children to be careful playing outside since an angry Chaneque might just kidnap them.

As we increasingly modernize, we move further and further away from folklore and the possibility of magic. I believe we have become guarded and jaded at our own expense; at the very least, we have locked down our imaginations and forfeited some creativity. This book invites you up to the attic of your mind where there's a treasure chest of fancies waiting to be opened. Shutter yourself away from the noises of today, light a candle or two, grab a cuddly blanket, sip a hot beverage, and unfasten the latch from your treasure chest. Savor the hygge moments of the holidays.

Sources:

The Alux and the Chaneque, Mexico's Elusive Elves
http://mexicounexplained.com/alux-chaneque-mexicos-elusive-elves/

Mythical Creatures Catalogue: Chaneque
https://www.mythicalcreaturescatalogue.com/post/2016/06/06/chaneque-mexico

Legend of the Nisse and Tomte
https://www.ingebretsens.com/culture/traditions/legend-of-nisse-and-tomte

Recipes

Christmas Congo Bars

1 stick margarine
1 cup quick oats
2 cups brown sugar
½ cup dark chocolate chips
3 eggs
½ cup dried cranberries or cherries
1 box red velvet cake mix
½ cup chopped walnuts (optional)

Melt butter. Add brown sugar. Cool.

Beat the eggs but don't overdo it.

Add the other items. (This is a very stiff batter)

Mix. Put in greased 9x13 pan.

Bake at 350° for 45 mins to 1 hour: The top will be hard and cracked in places.

Cut into bars while still warm.

We like to reheat individual bars in the microwave for a few seconds on day 2 and 3. Best eaten within two or three days of baking.

Raspberry Snow Bars

¾ cup shortening
¼ cup sugar
¼ tsp salt
¼ tsp almond extract
1½ cup flour
1 cup raspberry jam
½ cup coconut
½ cup sugar
2 eggs, separated

Preheat oven to 350°
Cream shortening, salt and ¼ cup sugar until fluffy.
Blend in almond extract and 2 egg yolks.
Mix in flour.
Pat dough into bottom of 9 x 13 pan.
Bake 15 minutes.
Spread hot crust with jam; top jam with coconut.
Beat egg whites until foamy, gradually beat in ½ cup sugar until stiff peaks form.
Spread the meringue over coconut.
Bake 25 minutes. Cool on rack.
Use a wet knife, non-stick knife, or knife sprayed with cooking spray to cut apart.

Mom's Molasses Crinkles

2¼ cups flour
1 cup packed brown sugar
2 tsp baking soda
1 egg
¼ tsp salt
¾ cup shortening
1 tsp cinnamon
⅓ cup full flavor molasses
1 tsp ground ginger
Sugar for topping
½ tsp ground cloves

Stir all dry ingredients together and set aside.
Cream shortening, molasses, sugar and egg thoroughly.
Add dry ingredients with mixer or by hand.
Chill dough for about two hours.
Shape dough into one inch balls.
Dip tops in sugar.
Bake on ungreased baking sheet at 350° for about 12
minutes.

Scandinavian Cut-outs

3¾ cups flour
1½ cup margarine
1¼ tsp baking powder
2 cups brown sugar, packed
⅛ tsp salt
1 egg
2½ tsp cinnamon
Your favorite glaze or icing
1¼ tsp ground cloves
½ tsp ground cardamom

Stir the dry ingredients together in one bowl

In another bowl: Cream margarine, adding brown sugar gradually until fluffy

Mix in egg until well-blended

Gradually stir in dry ingredients

Chill dough for at least 2 hours

Roll onto silicone mat or floured surface, about ⅛ inch thick.

Cut with floured cutters.

Bake on ungreased baking sheet at 350° for about 6 minutes until pale brown.

Ice or glaze to your desire.

Risengrød
(Danish Rice Pudding to leave for your nisse)

1 cup short-grained white rice pudding rice
½ cup water
1 quart milk
1 tsp salt
1 Tbsp vanilla extract or 2 whole beans
Cinnamon sugar
4 Tbsp sugar
1 Tbsp cinnamon

Pour the water and the rice in a large pot. Add salt, heat to a boil and allow to boil for about 2 minutes.

Pour the milk into the pot and let it boil while stirring.

Let the rice pudding boil lightly/simmer for about 35 minutes under a lid. Remember to stir the pudding regularly so that the rice does not burn and stick to the bottom of the pot. Add vanilla extract or cook 2 whole vanilla beans with the pudding and take out pods when done cooking, leaving the seeds in the pudding.

Mix the sugar and cinnamon in a small bowl.

Serve the rice pudding with a tablespoon of butter and the cinnamon sugar. Makes 3 servings. For a fun Christmas Eve treat, make the Risengrød, then add chopped toasted almonds (½ cup) to the pudding when finished. Serve with a warm fruit sauce and whipped cream. Add one whole almond tucked inside the pudding to one of the dishes before serving. According to tradition, the person who finds the whole almond gets a gift.

Victorian Christmas Fruit (decorative only)

Whole fruit, unpeeled: I like to use oranges, lemons and pears

Whole cloves (you need a lot!)

Poke the surface of each piece of fruit with a round toothpick so it is easier to insert cloves. Insert the cloves into the holes, leaving just the heads showing.

Insert a hook at the top that will take the weight of your fruit. I have used a heavy large paper clip.

Use a velvet ribbon to hang or you can place the fruit in a lovely bowl for a centerpiece.

Your studded fruit will make your house smell divine for weeks.

Victorian Cones (for treats or ornaments)

8x8 or 12x12 heavyweight decorative papers of choice
Ribbon or baker's twine

Place the square paper wrong side up, with a point facing down, so it looks sort of like a diamond. Draw an arc from the left point to the right point, and cut along that line.

Shape the paper into a cone, overlap the edges, and glue in place with strong craft glue. If you use solid paper, you can use a paper doily to cover the cone, which will make it look lacy.

Now have fun decorating it: lace, washi tape, gems, stickers.

For the handle, punch two holes in the top across from each other, thread ribbon through, and tie at the sides.

I like to fill these with candy or nuts and give them away.

Thank you to my Editor

The old dilemma of searching for an editor reared its ugly three heads, like Cerberus guarding the Underworld, forever in chains and angry as heck about it. Where could I find an editor who appreciates my story, who understands my voice, and who is nit-picky about the most minuscule of details? Look no further than a person who shares my DNA! My sister, Kay Rettenmund, agreed to edit this book before it was a book, although she deemed herself unworthy to do so, afraid she wasn't up to the task. Her skills are worth their weight in gold, or at least in pixie dust with extra sparkles! Thank you, dear sister, for helping to make this book print-worthy. Thank you for spending valuable time on the arduous task of validating the timeline and other logistics of the storyline. Thank you for enjoying the story no matter how many times you read it. Collaborating on the details was a special bonding experience for me and helped ease the doldrums of 2020 quarantine. I love you and wish I could pay you what you're worth.

Other titles in

the Deep Lakes Cozy Mystery Series

(Available from many independent bookstores, TEN16 Press, and online at Amazon, Barnes & Noble, and Target.)

The winter slumber of Deep Lakes, Wisconsin conceals dark secrets, awakened when the local pastor is found dead in his ice fishing shanty. Baker/vintner Frankie Champagne, owner of Bubble and Bake, is bent on proving her journalism chops and investigates the strange death. What could possibly go wrong as Frankie cuts her teeth on her first reporting gig, bringing to light secrets that were meant to stay in the darkness?

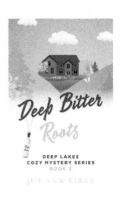

The promise of Spring in Deep Lakes, Wisconsin brings the community out of hibernation to plan the annual Roots Festival. Bubble and Bake owner Frankie Champagne just wants to help the Granite Mansion quarry heiress plan the keynote presentation. So, why does she find herself in the middle of the legendary and deadly Quarry Curse?

About the Author

Joy Ann Ribar lives in central Wisconsin where she writes the Deep Lakes Mystery Series, starring baker/vinter Frankie Champagne. Joy's writing is inspired by Wisconsin's four distinct seasons and other Wisconsin whimsical quirks, which she hopes to promote for all the world to enjoy. Joy is a member of Sisters in Crime, Blackbird Writers, and Wisconsin Writers Association. She enjoys researching viticulture at area wineries, chatting with readers, and meeting authors. Joy and her husband, John, someday plan to sell their house, buy an RV and travel around the U.S. spreading good cheer and hygge! Joy is a little proud that her first mystery, *Deep Dark Secrets*, was the #1 bestselling fiction with TEN16 Press, a division of Orange Hat Publishing, for 2019.

Sign up for email updates and see more about upcoming events at joyribar.com.
Follow Joy at: blackbirdwriters.com
Instagram: @authorjoyribar
Facebook: Joy Ann Ribar Wisconsin Author
            Blackbird Writers

If you enjoyed this book, please pass it along!
Leave a rating and review on:
Amazon.com
Goodreads.com
BookBub.com

CPSIA information can be obtained
at www.ICGtesting.com
Printed in the USA
JSHW050847231020
8971JS00004B/15